Salt Rain

a novel by Sarah Armstrong

Salt Rain

a novel by Sarah Armstrong

MacAdam/Cage

MacAdam/Cage
155 Sansome Street, Suite 550
San Francisco, CA 94104
www.macadamcage.com

Library of Congress Cataloging-in-Publication Data

Armstrong, Sarah, 1968-
  Salt rain / by Sarah Armstrong.
     p. cm.
  ISBN 1-59692-173-0 (alk. paper)
  I. Title.
  PR9619.4.A764S25 2006
  823'.92—dc22

                                   2006000694

Manufactured in the United States of America.

10 9 8 7 6 5 4 3 2 1

Book and cover design by Dorothy Carico Smith.

For Marion and Dick Armstrong

chapter one

The rain began as the train pulled slowly up the coast, through the small towns and dairy farms. It fell lightly at first, then descended as if a solid mass of water, sweeping across the hillsides of banana palms and bowing the cows' heads where they stood in the lush paddocks.

Every tree sliding by was a marker of the distance stretching between Allie and her mother, stretching thinner with every moment. Taking her further from their small terrace house where her mother would bucket hot water into their outdoor bathtub late at night, glowing mosquito coils scattered around the garden. Where her mother would climb naked out the bedroom window onto the roof to watch the sun rise over the city.

'Sure you don't want a rock cake?' Allie's aunt leaned over the armrest and offered the creased brown paper bag again.

'No. I hate them.' Allie turned to look out the window and in the reflection, watched crumbs dropping onto her aunt's shirt as she ate.

'Oh? These are pretty good,' said Julia. 'Wouldn't win anything at the Show though. See how the sultanas are mostly near the bottom?' She pointed with a thick finger then held the last of the cake high in the air and twirled it back and forth. 'You know, I used to be a judge at the Show a few years ago. The youngest judge ever, until they discovered I was doing it completely randomly.'

Allie hated her aunt for seeing right into her one moment of doubt and using it to bustle her onto the train. They had been in the kitchen after breakfast, teacups draining on the sink, the table wiped clean between them and Allie ready to leave for school, when Julia started telling her what the policeman had said. There were just words stringing their way through the air, until suddenly Allie couldn't breathe. It was as if the room had filled with water and they were sitting across the table from each other, eyes wide, holding their breath underwater. And somehow she had agreed to pack a bag and get on the train.

'Hey,' Julia's hand was warm on her arm, 'I'm going up to the buffet car. Do you want a sausage roll or something?'

Allie shook her head and kept her eyes fixed on the passing landscape as the train slowed and the paddocks gave way to a town. The rain overflowed in curtains from the gutters of small weatherboard houses and tall weeds grew high and luxuriant against back fences. She imagined her mother holed up in a town like this, sleeping in, then eating Chinese takeaway in her motel room.

Only the week before, her mother had gone to

Central station and got on the first train to come along. She told Allie that the old rattler took her west, through the new brick housing estates and high up into the Blue Mountains where she could see out over the red-roofed suburbs of Sydney. That evening, sitting up at the red Formica table in the kitchen, chopping onions for dinner, Mae described how she'd got off at Lithgow to catch a train back to the city, back to Allie. She had stood waiting on the cold platform, breathing the diesel fumes and the smell of coal from the mines while the carriages shunted and groaned beside her and she wished she could get back onto her train and coast down on to the western plains, that great free expanse of land, stretching all the way to the desert.

Julia took her seat again. 'That was Grafton we just went through. I always imagined it a much bigger place. Funny.'

From the corner of her eye, Allie watched her aunt sipping the paper cup of tea. There was nothing of her mother in Julia's long thin nose and rosy cheeks, even though they shared the same blood. Mae was creamy and elegant. Julia was tall and moved like a man and seemed so much older than she was. In Sydney she kept bumping into the furniture and doorways in the tiny house, her work boots loud on the floorboards.

Allie turned away and pressed her forehead hard against the cool glass of the window. The last time she had made the same trip, years ago, it was Mae beside her. Her mother had traced a long finger down the window, along the lines of rain tearing thin in the wind. Allie reached out a hand to do the same. Reflected in the glass was the curved collar of her school blouse that her mother had ironed on the weekend. She shut her eyes, every muscle in her body resisting the motion of the swaying train as it carried her northwards.

At the small train station, she ran across the platform to the shelter of the tin roof, the raindrops bursting on her hot skin and working their way under her clothes. Julia waited for the guard to pass the big suitcase from the boxcar, the rain plastering her long hair flat to her head.

Allie turned to a man in a blue uniform and shouted over the sound of the rain, 'When's the next train to Sydney?'

'Goin' back so soon?' He had missed some of his whiskers when he shaved. 'Not until the day after tomorrow,' he said. 'No passenger train till then, love.'

'What time does it go?'

'One o'clock.'

Julia was beckoning to her, shielding her eyes from the rain. Allie stepped out from the shelter of the verandah and followed her aunt across the gravel car park, over the puddles and carpet of bruised purple jacaranda flowers.

'Hop in if you like. Get in out of the rain.' Julia lifted their bags into the boot of the car. 'I'll finish loading up.'

Allie sat in the front seat, water still sliding down her skin, and looked over the train tracks at the people hurrying down the main street, under the long rows of palm trees. The first time she saw the palms, she had thrilled to their thin ribbed trunks and wild bursts of fronds. When she and Mae went home to Sydney, she had longed to return and look up at the line of palm trees and breathe the humid air, thick with sugar from the mills.

Julia slammed the boot and strode around the car. 'We could be in for some serious weather,' she said as she got in and leaned forward to wipe the foggy windscreen with her sleeve. 'The guard reckons there's a cyclone up north. We might catch the tail end of it. What were you talking to the stationmaster about?'

Allie watched the train gliding away. 'I'm going back on Thursday.'

'What do you mean?'

'I mean I'm going home.'

'I know you don't want to be here but you can't stay down there on your own. You're fourteen!' Julia's voice softened, 'What was I to do? Really, what was I to do?' She paused. 'You know…'

'But she'll come home, Julia. She'll get home and I won't be there! The house will be empty. How will she know where I am?' She saw the little terrace house as it was when Julia had hurried her out to the taxi, the beds stripped and curtains drawn.

'Allie,' Julia turned to look at her, 'I don't think Mae's coming back. The police…'

'How do they know?' Her aunt's eyes were suddenly too much like her mother's. 'What would any of you know about her? You haven't seen her for years. She's just taken off to clear her head.' She reached for the doorhandle, but couldn't bear more rain on her skin. 'Tom drives her mad sometimes… she always comes back.'

'It's been three nights.'

'I already told you! They had a fight. Even she says it, that she always runs away when things get difficult.'

'I know,' Julia sighed. 'Mae's always run away.'

'And she always comes back!'

Julia kneaded the steering wheel. 'Her clothes were on the seat of the dinghy...'

'She always skinny-dips! See, you don't know her at all!'

Julia nodded and started the car. 'Let's just go home and have something to eat... eh?'

Allie shook her head and looked out the window as her aunt drove them through town, over the wide brown river and towards the mountains, the rain drumming relentlessly on the roof of the car and stirring the fields of sugar cane, bending the tall stalks in waves. It was the very same rain that had fallen on her mother's skin before Allie was born, the raindrops making an endless circuit from earth to clouds, the same water falling again and again for decades. She touched her tongue to the back of her hand and tried to remember the taste of her mother's skin.

Julia drove with her legs wide and her hand resting on the column shift. The car ground slowly up the steep hairpin bends, each turn revealing the river winding across the floodplain below.

Allie spoke into the silence, 'The police have obviously got no idea what a good swimmer she is.'

Julia nodded. 'You're right. They probably don't...' She wound her window down a crack. 'You know, she used to swim up and down the waterhole for hours. She said the eels nipped her. It made me too scared to go in.'

Allie thought of Mae's arms curving neatly into the water. On unbearably hot summer nights, the two of them would go down to the harbour to swim off one of the industrial wharves. Mae would skip ahead, swinging her towel and shouting, her voice echoing around the dark warehouses shut up for the night, 'To swim! To swim!' Allie would paddle close to the ladder, listening to the waves slapping into the massive wooden piers and watching Mae swim way out into the darkness of the harbour, her pale arms flashing over the black water. Later, they ran home through the narrow streets, the tar road warm and soft under their bare feet and their towels flapping from their shoulders like capes. Allie would wake in the morning and find the sheets and mattress damp from her wet hair and swimming costume.

'She taught me how to swim, you know,' she said to Julia. 'The guy at the pool said she could be a swimming teacher and he'd give her a job.'

'I bet he did!' Julia started to say something else then shook her head. 'Oh, Mae.'

She glared at her aunt. 'So, can you swim as well as her?'

Julia changed gears as they reached the top of the hill. She turned to Allie and shook her head.

It was the same as last time, the dirt road winding into the narrow valley and the forest coming right down to the vivid green paddocks. The rain started to fall even harder and the car filled with the sound of the windscreen wipers beating back and forth. Julia stopped at a small weatherboard shop with a faded Coke sign in the window and a knot of kids in bright raincoats waiting under the shelter of the verandah. She reached for the car door. 'Why don't you come in with me? I'm going to pick up a couple of things. You could see if there's anything special you'd like. Chocolate or chips…'

'No.'

Julia slammed the door behind her and hurried through the rain to the shop.

Allie had forgotten the way the wet heat of the valley entered her body and slowly rose through her, as if heating and swelling her insides. She remembered the sweat beading on her mother's skin when they came up last time, small trembling balls of moisture on her upper lip and neck. Perhaps Mae had taken the train over the Blue Mountains all the way to the desert, perhaps she was standing on the hot red dirt this very minute, looking out into the shimmering nothingness.

The back door of the car opened and a woman got in, piling bags of shopping onto the seat. 'So, I'm Petal,' she said. She had a tanned face and blonde hair pinned up on her head.

'Hello.' Allie could smell something sweet, like the joss sticks Mae bought in Chinatown once.

'You're with Julia.'

'She's my aunt. She's my mother's younger sister.'

'Oh. I never knew Julia had a sister. I thought she was an only child.' Petal began rummaging in her things, taking out bulging brown paper bags and scraps of twisted paper. 'So, where do you live? I haven't seen you around.'

'Sydney. I'm only staying until Thursday.' Allie could see the curve of Petal's breasts through her thin shirt. Mae didn't care if the neighbours saw her naked on the roof. An old man who lived in a boarding house across the back lane would watch from his window. 'It's my gift to him,' Mae used to say.

'Only till Thursday?' said Petal. 'Uh oh. I hope it stops raining for you then. They say the wet season's going to be early this year. But you must have been here lots of times. Your family's an institution in this place. Here it is!' She pulled out a jar of dark golden honey, still flecked with wax. 'This is unbelievable, it's from the rainforest.' She unscrewed the lid, 'Stick your finger in. Taste it.'

Allie was surprised at how thick the honey was. She shut her eyes to the intense sweetness and the sensation of sucking on her finger. There, in the muggy car, with the spicy damp smell of the woman and the drumming rain, she felt certain that her mother was starting to make her way home.

Petal touched the back of Allie's neck with a sticky finger. 'Look how you're sweating. Julia never swims in the waterholes, she says the water's too murky. But if you want, I'll take you down for a swim before you go. There's a path from our side of the creek.'

Allie nodded, the sensation of Petal's finger lingering on her skin.

A big white school bus pulled up and the kids ran out to climb on, slipping in the mud. An old man and child got off the bus and stepped slowly over the puddles. The man, in a long brown raincoat and felt hat, glanced at the car, and then stopped, pausing in the rain to look again, his eyes narrowing. He walked along the verandah of the shop, and turned to look back from the doorway.

'He's looking at you,' said Petal. 'You must know

him, do you? Old Clarry.' She screwed the lid back on the jar.

'No. I've only been here once before. Who is he?'

'One of the original valley folk, owns a property back that way.' She motioned with her head up the valley. 'He spends most of his time babysitting these days. He buggered his back.' She bit into a small red apple. 'So you've only been here once, huh?'

Julia got back in the car and passed Allie a paper bag to hold.

'Old Clarry was just looking at your niece like he'd seen a ghost,' said Petal.

'Oh, really? Where you'd spring from, Petal?' Julia smiled over her shoulder.

'I was hoping you'd give me a lift. Thought I'd have to walk the rest of the way home in the bloody rain.'

'No worries,' said Julia as she started the car.

'Where have you been? I dropped in to see you yesterday.'

'Sydney.' Julia pulled out around the bus.

'Can anyone take the bus?' Allie asked.

Julia frowned at Allie.

'Yeah,' said Petal. 'I take it to town sometimes. You've got to put up with all the kids though. Julia, you went to Sydney? Really? Why?'

'What time does it come by?' said Allie.

'Twice in the morning,' said Petal. 'At about seven and then at eight. One run for the primary school and one for the high school. Do you like catching buses?'

'I need to get to town in a couple of days.'

Julia sighed. 'You know you can't, Allie. It's just not…'

Allie clenched her teeth and looked out at the rain moving in curtains along the high valley walls. 'You can't stop me, you know. Mae will be bloody furious when she finds out.'

Petal leaned forward. 'Who's Mae? Your mum?'

'Just drop it, Petal.' Julia braked suddenly to cross a low cement bridge.

'Okay, okay. Keep your pants on, love. Hey, did you know your car is leaking back here? There's water coming in the door seal.'

'Yeah. I know it.'

Petal wound down the window and threw her apple core out into the rushing brown water. 'Oh well, it matches everything else at your place then. Look how high the creek is already.'

Allie turned in her seat to face Petal, her back to Julia. 'Will it flood?'

'Yes,' said Julia. 'It floods every year. But we won't have a big one for a while yet, there's not enough water in the soil. Maybe later, after Christmas.'

When Allie was younger, she and her mother used to lie in bed listening to the rain and imagining the great flood that would come. They planned to wait in their hilltop terrace house, watching the whole city go under, then they would launch their dinghy from the roof and paddle around the vast new sea.

'Like the flood when I was born?' she said.

Julia glanced over at Allie. 'So you know about that?'

'She tells me everything.' She stared back at her aunt, 'Everything about the valley.'

'Oh, is that right?' Julia smiled as she turned the car up a muddy rutted driveway. 'Hey Petal, there'll be heaps of eggs in the chook house. Go grab some if you want.' She looked sideways at Allie. 'Do you remember collecting eggs when you came up for Dad's funeral? You really loved the chooks.'

'Yeah. I remember.' She was eight years old and she had sat up beside her aunt at the kitchen table, helping wrap each smooth brown egg in a piece of newspaper and packing it into a small cardboard box. She had carefully carried the box onto the train, thinking of the plump hens scratching at their straw. Halfway home, Mae had taken the box from her and dumped it into one of the rubbish bins and Allie had quietly cried for the golden yolks the chickens had made for her.

She hardly recognised the farmhouse for the trees and bushes growing up against the walls and over the rusted tin roof. Last time, the cows had grazed the pasture right up to a neat wire fence around the house.

Straggly hydrangea bushes wiped against her legs as she followed Julia up the cracked cement path, past the fence, rusting where it lay in the waist-high grass. Mae would laugh when Allie told her that purple fluffy-topped weeds were blooming in the cracks between the verandah boards.

'They'll be mad at me for leaving them for so long,' said Julia, looking over to where Petal was opening the door of the chicken shed, the birds clucking indignantly. 'I'll take them some green stuff later.' She banged the front door open with her hip.

Inside, there was the sour smell of mould and every flat surface was stacked with books and papers and glass jars of what looked like dust.

'Seeds. They're seeds,' said Julia, as Allie bent to look

at one of the jars. 'I'm helping the forest reclaim its land.' She waved her hand towards the paddock outside the window and walked through into the next room.

The place was even messier than last time. A vine curled in an open window by the front door, its fine green tendrils reaching for the curtain rod, and blue work shirts hung on a line sagging across the room. Last visit, Mae had stopped at the front door as if reluctant to step inside, then she had walked slowly through every room in the house, trailing her fingers over the walls and the heavy dark furniture, leaving shiny tracks in the dust and collecting spider webs on her fingertips.

'You're in here.' Julia put one of Allie's bags in Mae's old room, with its two narrow single beds. She touched the toe of her boot to the puddle on the floor. 'I'd better get you a bucket for that leak.'

From the window Allie watched Petal walking across the paddock under a red umbrella, past dozens of small trees growing up through green plastic tree guards. Petal closed the umbrella, then bent to climb through the wire fence and disappeared into the tall forest. Allie didn't recall the forest being so dark or close to the house.

Julia sat down on one of the beds. 'I'll make some space for you in the wardrobe. There's some old dresses of Mae's in there you might like to wear. They should fit you.'

'I'm not staying, Julia.'

'Allie? I'm just trying to be realistic…'

Her voice was loud. 'You know where she is? She's in some hotel down south. She's staying down there and getting herself together. She's done it before.'

'You never said she'd left you alone overnight.'

'I never said she didn't!' She paused, 'She's only done it once or twice.'

Julia shook her head, and spoke quietly, 'Listen to me. She's not at some country pub. They found her dinghy. It's just a matter of time…'

'It's not her dinghy! It's my dinghy. And what gives you the right to make me stay up here? You're not my mother.'

Julia looked down at her feet. 'You know what the police said.'

'No! That's just what you want. I know you were always jealous that she got away from the valley and you never did. Because you were never brave enough to leave.'

'What?' Julia's eyes widened. 'Is that what she told you?' She got up awkwardly and stood in the doorway, shaking her head. 'Oh, that's rich. That's bloody rich, that is.' She walked out, her boots heavy on the floorboards.

Allie sat down on the bed that she knew had been Mae's when she was a girl. Everything was damp, the blanket under her and her school blouse sticking to her hot skin. She lay down and rolled over to face the wall. The house shook as Julia banged open the swollen wooden door onto the back verandah.

The first night that Mae ever stayed away, Allie had sat up in the dark kitchen, her senses tuned to the faintest noise or movement as she waited the night through. She never spoke to anyone about it, not her teacher when she took herself to school in the morning and not even to Mae when she found her mother sitting on the back step in the afternoon, smoking and reading a magazine, the oars laid out on the kitchen floor, ready for a row on the harbour.

The day they got the dinghy was Allie's ninth birthday. Mae had woken her early and the sun was just starting to rise as they let themselves out of the house and walked down the empty streets. At the wharves, fishermen in gumboots hosed down boat decks and wheeled crates along the dock. Inside, they skated boxes of fish and ice over the floor, shouting across the room to each other, and there was the sharp smell of raw fish. It was embarrassing the way men noticed Mae, heads turning to watch her pass.

After a few minutes a tall man with a thin red face came over and stood beside her. 'Mae,' he said and started to roll a cigarette.

'Hey George.'

'I've got it down at the wharf for you. You still want it then?'

'Uh huh,' Mae nodded and reached for his pouch of tobacco. He smiled and handed her his just-rolled cigarette and leaned forward to light it for her.

'So, this is your daughter?'

'This is Allie. It's her birthday.' Mae's warm hand rested on her shoulder.

He smiled at Allie. 'You like fish?'

She liked crumbed fish fingers but not the whole fish with dead eyes that Mae sometimes brought home and baked in the oven.

'Go and pick one, love. From that box over there.' He pointed, 'Go on. It's okay.'

She walked over and stood before the box and then

turned back to look at Mae. The man and her mother watched her, smiling. She looked down at the slimy skin and glistening eyes. Then he was behind her. 'That one?' he pointed.

She nodded.

He picked it up and wrapped it in paper and gave it to her. 'Come on. Let's go get your birthday present, Miss Allie.'

At the wharf, seagulls screamed, rising and falling with the wind, orange legs extended. The small tin dinghy floated down below, a puddle under its wooden bench seat.

'You can leave her at my mooring if you want, Mae. You know where it is. You'd best take the oars with you, though. I might be able to find somewhere for you to leave them. But take them today.' He stood with his legs wide and arms crossed.

Mae smiled up at him. 'You're a winner George. It's perfect.'

'Whatever you say, Mae. Whatever you say, darlin'.' He rested his hand on her cheek for a moment.

They walked back through the streets, Mae holding the oars across her shoulders and Allie carrying the heavy fish. At home, Mae leaned the oars behind the door in the laundry.

'Can we row out to one of the harbour islands for a picnic?' Allie asked.

'Sure, sweetheart. Of course.' Mae washed her hands at the laundry tub.

'Can we take Clare from school with us? I owe her a visit to my house.'

Mae turned off the tap. 'Let's make it our secret. Just you and me. You won't say anything to Tom, will you? Let's not share it with Clare or Tom or anyone.'

Allie didn't see the fisherman again until he appeared at the front door the morning that Mae disappeared. He stood beside the policeman, the two of them silhouetted in the sunlight.

In the afternoon, she stood at the bedroom window and watched her aunt wheel a barrow of saplings down the long slope to the bottom paddock. Julia had trampled the weeds to make paths to the newly planted trees. All signs of the cows were gone, except for the old dairy building and a tractor, streaked brown with rust and abandoned in the house paddock.

Soon she would be sitting on the train again, watching the landscape change back to dry eucalyptus and sandstone, gliding alongside the Hawkesbury River where oyster frames break the glassy surface. Mae would be waiting for her in their little kitchen, wearing one of her sundresses, her hands around a steaming teacup.

Julia disappeared behind the high weeds and there was just the wind scattering rain across the tin roof and a distant cow lowing. Allie had heard quiet crying from Julia's room earlier in the day and the memory of it turned her guts to ice in the heavy afternoon heat.

She found a pair of muddy gumboots on the verandah and hurried down the stairs and through the wet grass, the oversized boots slapping her calves with every step. She was surprised by the wave of relief she felt when she saw Julia bending to pick up a potted tree.

Her aunt looked up and stood with her hands on her hips as Allie hurried through the sticky weeds towards her.

'What are you doing?' Allie was breathless.

'See this one I'm planting now?' Julia pointed with her chin as she picked up the shovel again and pushed it into the ground with her boot. 'In a hundred years its trunk will reach from here over to the wheelbarrow.'

Allie's throat tightened at the sight of the red soil. Rusty red like dried blood, spilling onto the luminous grass.

'This whole farm will be rainforest again. Even the house, I hope.' Julia smiled as she tipped the sapling from its pot and slid it into the hole. 'I'm letting the forest take its own back. Letting natural order re-establish itself.'

Allie turned to look at the sea of tree guards and tall weeds bending with the weight of the rain. 'And what then?'

'Huh?'

'When the forest has taken it back, what then?'

Julia shrugged, smiling. 'Then my job will be done. I won't be needed anymore.'

'But look at it!' Allie waved her arm around. 'It's nothing like rainforest. It looked better before, when the cows were still here.'

Julia nodded slowly. 'Yeah. Well, there are some in the valley who'd agree with you. Your great-uncle, for instance. And your great-grandmother.' She flicked her long plait over her shoulder as she bent to scoop soil around the tree roots. 'But it's my farm to do what I want with. And I know the forest will reclaim it eventually anyway. I'm just helping it. See, here's one that came up on its own.' She tenderly moved the long grass from around a seedling. 'A sandpaper fig. There must have been a huge one right here somewhere, until my father or grandfather cut it down.' She turned and started digging another hole. 'That seed was in the soil the whole time, just waiting for a safe time to grow.'

Allie squatted and stroked the leaves of the tiny tree.

Julia stopped digging. 'Did Mae really say that about me?'

'Say what?'

'That I wasn't brave enough to leave the valley. That I wasn't as brave as her.'

Allie rubbed the hairy leaf between her fingers. No-one was brave like Mae. Allie was terrified whenever Mae took her out into the middle of the dark harbour. She used to stay in the rocking dinghy, hands gripping the thin tin sides while Mae somersaulted and dived, her white legs disappearing under the glinting waves.

She looked up at Julia. 'Why didn't you leave?'

Julia rolled up a sleeve on her faded blue shirt before she spoke. 'There's nothing special about leaving somewhere.'

'She says that brave is just a choice you make and some people don't make it.'

Julia nodded. 'Yeah? Perhaps. And maybe the bravest choices just don't look that way.' She turned back to her digging.

Allie stared at her aunt's back, then snapped the leaf off and took a handful of the red soil. She closed her fist tight and the sticky clay squeezed out between her fingers. Her mother's childish sandal might have pressed for a moment on this very piece of earth as she ran down the paddock in her school dress. Allie imagined Mae running, the cotton of her dress straining against the warm air, the sun stinging her arms, and him too, of course he would have been there, the First Love. Mae and the First Love, both of them descending through the thick summer air to the creek.

'Where's the First Love?'

'Huh?' Julia kept digging. 'What's the first love?'

'Mum's First Love. The boy she loved.'

'Do you mean Saul Philips?' Julia turned to her, frowning.

'Saul,' Allie repeated. It wasn't right somehow. Why did Mae never tell her his name?

'Why do you ask?'

'Where is he?'

Julia's wet boot slipped off the shovel. 'Shit!' She stood up and rubbed her hands on the seat of her overalls. 'I don't keep track of him. He's probably at his house or over at his father's place, working.'

So the First Love was still in the valley, his cells still holding traces of their first kiss down by the creek, where the cicadas had been so loud around them that they couldn't talk. Mae had told Allie her surprise at the heat of his tongue in her mouth and how a rash had spread over his chest and neck as they walked home that first day, great blotches rising red on his skin, that his father had called heat rash and treated with calamine lotion.

'Where does he live?'

Julia's brow furrowed. 'Up the end of the valley, on the back section of his dad's property.' She picked up another sapling.

'Where up the end of the valley?'

'Why are you so interested? That was all years ago, you know.'

'He makes those wire things, right?'

Julia turned back to Allie and raised her eyebrows. 'How do you know about them? Have you met him?'

'No. Mae told me.'

'Oh. Well, yes. He does still make them.' Julia looked at Allie for a long moment, then bent down to plant the tree.

chapter two

After dinner, Julia sat at the kitchen table writing out the day's plantings in her diary. Red cedar, quandong, white lilly pilly, native tamarind. She liked to imagine the forest slowly enfolding the farm while she slept, the mottled trunks swelling with sap and vines snaking in the windows.

It was still light outside, the only sounds her pencil whispering across the paper and insects flying into the window panes. Allie was in one of the cane chairs on the verandah, her arms wrapped around her knees, looking out at the forest. When Julia got to Sydney she had reached for Allie, wanting to wrap that small body up and protect her from what she guessed was coming, but the girl had pushed her away, surprisingly fierce. On the train down to the city Julia had stupidly imagined her as the eight-year-old she had met years before at the farm, but when Julia walked in the open front door of the tiny terrace house, Allie was lying on the couch in the bare living room, her eyes shut, arms flung above her head, a young woman with long dark hair and a face frighteningly like Mae's. The same beautiful face.

Julia spread out her big hand-drawn map of the farm and carefully drew a symbol for each tree she had planted that day. In Mae's narrow hallway, the policeman had unfolded his map of the harbour, his voice quiet as he moved his finger across the crazy curves of the foreshore. 'This is where we are looking. And this is where the people on the ferry saw her.' He spoke to her as if she was familiar with this Mae who lived in a dingy house, who had erotic books beside her bed and a wardrobe full of silky dresses. He spoke as if she knew Tom, in his sharply creased dark suit, leaning against the counter in the kitchen, his impatience with the police obvious. She was thankful that Tom didn't try to make eye contact. She was afraid he would see her thinking about Mae's phone call, hearing over and over again her sister's voice leaking from the handset into the dark farmhouse.

That first night in the city, she had lain awake in Mae's bed. There was too much noise, too many people, too close. She got up and sat on the chair by the open window, counting the lights being extinguished one by one in the dark buildings, marvelling at the lives of strangers unfolding so close to each other. Sitting there, waiting for the dawn, she knew that her mother had been right, she would never have survived in the city, after all. She had never imagined it so hard, so overwhelmingly treeless. She wondered if Mae had ever sat in that same chair and thought of Julia doing time on the farm, shovelling shit, heaving the cows in and out of the stalls and creeping past her father's door. Did Mae ever think about Julia growing older up in the valley, passing out of her teens, into her twenties, a farm wife before her time, a farm wife with no husband? Perhaps some people were simply destined to stay in the valley and some were meant to get away. Saul left, but he told her that for weeks before his father wrote to ask him to come home and help, he had dreamt of the valley every night, of flying slowly above the forest, then swooping down over the lush paddocks and the cows gathering at the dairy.

At the first glow of sun in the sky, the streetlights sputtered out and the tiny morning birds began flitting from rooftop to rooftop, their chirping thin and weak. Through the buildings, Julia could just see the harbour and how much darker and denser it was than the ocean or the river back home. The policeman had talked to her about the harbour currents and the way the water could sweep unpredictably from cove to cove.

Once the sun had risen and filled the attic bedroom, she knelt on the floor in front of Mae's wardrobe and swept her face back and forth across the dresses, then buried her face deep into the slippery silky fabric. She pressed it hard against her eyes and waited for the day to begin.

chapter three

Allie woke to Julia's voice loud on the phone in the hallway of the farmhouse, 'Okay. Okay. Don't worry, we'll get her across. Yep.'

She swung her legs to the edge of the bed, her heart hammering. It could be Mae on the phone, standing in a phone box on a wide empty street in some beach town, propping the door open with one leg, coins ready to drop in. And as she waited for Allie to come to the phone, she would be looking down to fishing boats leaving with the tide, like they saw in that town Tom took them to.

Julia turned on the hallway light and came to Allie's bedroom door wrapped in a sheet. She whispered, 'Are you awake?'

'Who was that on the phone?'

'A neighbour. I'm going down to the third crossing. The creek's up and I have to re-string the old flying fox. Do you want to come?'

The floor was gritty and damp under Allie's feet as she stepped into a pair of shorts and a T-shirt and followed her aunt out into the misty dawn air.

Julia drove slowly down the muddy driveway, steering the tyres either side of deep ruts. 'Marion—who lives up the valley—her baby's coming and there are problems. We need to get her across. They made three of these flying foxes to bring the bananas over, before the bridge was built. They'd hook a hand of 'nanas on and send it flying down from the shed up the top. But we used it for all sorts of things. The road used to go under all the time and we'd send food across to the Burns and the McAlisters in the big floods. Mum would do up parcels of corned beef and flour and sugar. The Burns were always hopeless at stocking up before the wet. But we haven't had a really big flood for ages. This is nothing, it'll be down by this afternoon, I bet. Still,' she turned to look at Allie, and smiled, 'you got your flood, sooner than I thought.'

They turned a corner and there was the churning creek. The road on each side sank down into the wide band of brown water that heaved with branches and dirty foam.

Allie looked back the way they had come. 'Is the road to town flooded too? Can I still get to town?' She pictured the train disappearing down the coast without her.

Julia turned off the engine and there was just the thundering of the creek. 'We only brought a person over once before, when the youngest Watson boy broke his leg. He came across, his leg in a splint, howling all the way.'

She waved to the two people getting out of the car on the other side then reached over to the back seat for her toolbox. Her voice was conversational, 'I won't just let you take off, you know. If you go, I'll follow you. Simple as that.' She got out and climbed up the bank to the thick wooden post of the flying fox, her toolbox hanging from one arm.

Allie opened the car door and crossed the muddy gravel to the edge of the forest. She peered into the dense tangled foliage. How easy it would be take a few steps, slip between the trees and disappear into the dimness. She would find her way over the hills and down onto the plain. She glanced over to see if Julia was watching her, just as a Land Rover pulled up and a grey-haired man got out, buttoning up a raincoat. He waved across the creek and stuck his thumb in the air. When he saw Allie he paused for a minute, and then smiled and called across to her as he climbed the embankment to Julia, 'Hi, I'm Michael. The doctor.'

'Hello,' Allie could hardly hear her own voice for the sound of the water.

The pregnant woman over the other side was carrying a striped umbrella as she walked slowly back and forth across the road, her belly jutting before her. Every few minutes she stopped and squatted on the rutted gravel. The man who was walking with her bent down and leaned in close while the umbrella trembled over them.

Allie went to the edge of the creek where it eddied onto the road and looked upstream, searching for the rock where Mae and the First Love had kissed, but all the boulders were hidden under the seamless rushing water. Mae had told her about the cracking sound the boulders made as they collided underwater, but there was only the tremendous roar of the water being sucked downstream and Julia's voice as she bellowed across the creek.

The man on the other side threw a rope across. It fell short and he retrieved it hand over hand from the pull of the water. Julia waded out knee-deep and the water ran up her side, so her clothes stuck to her stomach and heavy breasts. The man inched his car into the creek and stood on the bonnet, bracing his feet to throw the rope again. Julia caught it and they held it in the air, a sagging, dripping line stretching defiantly over the creek.

While Julia rethreaded the flying fox, her lips white with the effort of twisting the ends of the wire together, the woman walked back and forth on the other side, crying, her face contorted. The man carried the umbrella for her but she kept turning, suddenly changing direction and walking out from under its shelter into the drifting rain.

Allie wanted to capture it all, like a photo, for Mae. The forest growing right to the edge of the creek, the tendrils of mist caught on the trees, the brightly dressed woman under the umbrella and Julia frowning as she cut the wire.

She stepped closer to the forest and peered in, but could see only a few metres into the dense foliage. Mae had told her about the paths through the forest that she and the First Love had used to go between their houses. Allie wondered if he was awake, looking out at the misty clouds resting on the treetops. A stream of cool dank air came from the forest and brushed against her face. She stepped backwards and hurried over towards Julia as her aunt stood up and yelled across the creek for the man to get in the harness and come across, to test the wire.

The man's hands were shaking when he reached their side and undid the harness. He stepped off onto the dirt. 'Quick, get it back to her, Julia. She's not doing so well.'

When the woman got into the harness, she dropped her umbrella to the water's edge where it rocked from side to side. She was halfway across when the rain became torrential, the air suddenly thick with water. Allie shielded her eyes to watch the woman, who was swaying over the river, her body glowing in the silvery light.

Allie imagined her dropping into the rushing water and being sucked downstream. She wondered if the baby would sense it was in danger or if it would be in its element, tumbling and turning in the waters of its mother's womb as the river delivered them both to the ocean.

Mae used to tell her about the little Islander girl found floating way out in the middle of the Pacific Ocean. Allie couldn't remember the American sailor who had told Mae the story but she knew every detail of how he had traced the currents back to figure out which island the little girl came from. She knew how tiny the girl's body appeared from his big ship, just a piece of flotsam on the vast ocean. A motorboat was sent out to retrieve her body and the wake rippled her long hair and disturbed the phosphorescent fish nudging at her. The sailor said that when he reached down to pull her from the water, it took him a few moments to register that her body was warm and that she had opened her eyes and was staring up at him.

Julia and the man pulled hard on the rope and the

woman slid along the wire to safety. The two men carried her to the doctor's car and they drove off with a spray of gravel.

Julia threw the toolbox onto the back seat of the car and sat for a moment before she started the engine, rubbing the muddy fingers of her right hand. 'That's going to have to be done again, properly. That was a real bushman's job.' She reached down to pluck a leech off her leg and flicked it out the window. 'Michael was the doctor at your birth, you know.'

'The guy that was here just now?'

'Yeah.'

Allie's voice rose with indignation. 'Why didn't he say something?'

Julia shrugged. 'I guess he didn't know it was you or… I don't know. I'm sorry. I would have introduced you but I could see Marion was panicking. I was just trying to get the wires tied off and bring her over.'

Allie knew that the flood when she was born had nearly washed away the town and filled the little hospital with water. Countless times she had pictured the patients on their trolleys, leaving a wake as they were wheeled down the corridor, while all around them bandages and stethoscopes and vases of flowers bobbed in the muddy water. Mae's bed was an island, her legs in the air, her private parts covered with a sheet, the doctor standing at the end of the bed in his gumboots. That very doctor. Mae told her that the rain had been so loud on the tin roof that she couldn't hear herself scream. No-one came to visit her, not her own mother, not Julia. Not even the First Love. No-one except her teacher, Mrs Brickner, who brought five de-thorned yellow roses wrapped in a wet tissue and tinfoil and stayed for just five minutes. Mae had got up in the middle of the first night and waded up to the nursery to stand looking at the two babies lying in their cribs. Two babies born in a flood. She told Allie that she couldn't tell which was her baby. She couldn't even remember if she had birthed a boy or a girl.

While Julia was planting down the paddock, Allie walked from room to room of the house. When they had come up for her grandfather's funeral, it was unsettling to see her mother so at home there. Mae had moved confidently to a drawer in the wooden sideboard to get soup spoons, and when she lit the woodchip water heater for Allie's bath, she had reached without looking to the top of the bathroom cabinet for matches.

Allie knelt down and touched the floorboards, soft and satiny from the stroke of her mother's feet. Mae had walked across these boards the day she met him, and then on the day of the first kiss. Later, quietly, she had carried the hidden weight of Allie through this very room.

It was still raining, the clouds low over the house. Allie stood in the doorway to Julia's room and wished she were at the little fishing town down south, lying back on the burning white beach with Mae, their wet bodies caked with fine sand and shell grit. Mae had showed her how to dive down and claw her fingers into the sandy bottom while the waves crashed over them and dragged at their trailing legs. Perhaps Mae had gone back to the same motel and was stretched out on one of those sagging beds, gritty sand on the sheets and the sound of the ocean loud through the night.

Julia's bed was a square of patchwork in a sea of papers and books and jars of seeds. Allie looked inside the wardrobe but it was almost empty, just three pairs of worn jeans on hangers and work shirts folded neatly in a pile, her bras stacked, the big cups fitting into each other. Papers on the dressing table were weighted with river rocks, each one labelled in texta, *Seed Collection, Propagation* and *Local Weeds*. Allie picked up a notebook from the bedside table. The latest entry read, *Train tickets $100, taxis $25, tea on train $2.*

She had seen her mother setting off on one of her train trips once. Allie was coming home from school early and caught sight of Mae standing on the next platform at Circular Quay station, gently swinging her handbag as she waited. It was the look on her mother's face that had surprised her, the transparent excitement. Mae had once told her that catching random trains was the perfect kind of gambling. After her mother's train left, Allie had climbed the stairs to the other platform and went right to where her mother had stood. The next train to come along rattled its way out through the suburbs. She let her eyes blur the houses as she sped past, hundreds of people left behind, the train like an arrow to somewhere. She waited for the impulse to get off, wondering whether Mae did the same, standing by the carriage door, letting it begin to close before she slipped out onto the small station in the middle of bare cow paddocks. Allie stood at the end of the empty platform in the cool afternoon air and watched the train tracks disappearing into the distance.

There was the sound of someone walking up the verandah steps. Allie put Julia's notebook back and from the bedroom door watched Petal wipe her bare feet on the mat and step inside, letting the screen door bang behind her.

'Oh, there you are. Julia said you were up here. Do you want to come for a swim?'

'In the rain?'

'That's the best time. We'll go to one of the little side creeks.' Petal picked up one of the biscuits cooling on a cake rack and took a bite. 'She's such a good cook.'

'Brown sugar shortbreads. My mother makes them too.' She walked over to the table. Julia had forgotten to press a fork into the top of the pale discs. 'Can you explain to me where Saul lives?'

Petal smiled and brushed crumbs from around her mouth. 'What's your interest in Saul Philips?'

Allie could hear Julia coming in the back door. She picked up a warm shortbread and held it to her nose. 'Mae's got all her recipes in her head. She can only remember them when she's right there cooking. Once a neighbour asked her to write the fruitcake recipe down and she had to make it to remember it. When she was a girl she used to make a fruitcake for the Show every year. They each cooked one, her and Julia, to enter in the kid's section and everyone thought they cheated and got help from their mother and grandmother, but Mae said that they'd send them out of the kitchen onto the verandah and do it completely on their own.'

'Why do you call your mother Mae?'

Allie put the shortbread down. 'She prefers it.'

Julia spoke from the laundry door. 'She talked to you about our fruitcakes?'

Allie shrugged her shoulders. She had always felt

whispers of jealousy when Mae talked about Julia. 'Little Julia' she sometimes called her, even though Julia was taller than Mae and only two years younger.

'Why don't you enter anything in the Show now, Julia?' Petal picked up another shortbread.

Julia laughed as she dropped a basket of rough-skinned bush lemons onto the table. 'You think the judges pick the best cake, Petal? I was just formalising it by doing it randomly. My system was a lot fairer. The year that Mae and I won, Grandma must have been owed a favour.'

'Mae said you won heaps of times,' said Allie. 'She got first and you got second.'

Julia chewed on her bottom lip and tipped the lemons out. 'Well, it was a while ago...'

'It's good you're staying longer, Allie,' Petal said. 'They say you're not a real valley person until you've endured a wet season.'

'Who told you I'm staying longer?' Allie glared at her aunt.

Julia shook her head, her voice quiet, 'Don't, Allie... don't...'

'And how will you stop me, Julia? You have no right.'

Julia walked across to the kitchen sink and filled the kettle with water. 'She's a real valley person, Petal. She was born in a flood. If you like, Allie, we can go down to Sydney together in a few weeks. For a visit.' She turned the oven on. 'I'm making a lemon meringue pie. Do you want to squeeze the lemons?'

'You can't stop me!' Allie pushed past Petal and out onto the verandah. The next day, she would be down at the train station, buying her ticket home. Tom had

...llars on the day that Mae disappeared. ... pressed it into her hand in the kitchen ... with the policeman.

...d found her where she stood under ...ngo tree, rain dripping around her. 'So, are you coming for a swim?'

'I don't have my swimmers.'

Petal smiled and squeezed Allie's arm. 'Who said anything about swimmers?'

Inside the forest, it was cool and dark. She followed close behind Petal, along the narrow path layered thick with wet decaying leaves. There was the same dank earthiness she had smelt down at the creek and rain dripped on them from the high canopy of trees and looping vines. Birds fluttered through the branches as they passed. They came out onto a big boulder at the edge of a creek and Petal rolled up her towel and tucked it under a small rock overhang. 'What's going on with you and Julia?'

'She's just got something against my mum. She wants me to stay here. I guess she's lonely.'

'You reckon she's lonely?' Petal shucked off her dress and dived in. Her body was tanned and firm, different to Mae's soft voluptuousness. Allie counted out loud as Petal swam underwater to the far end of the waterhole. It was her job to time Mae as she swam the length of the local baths in one breath, her body an arrow, hair billowing with each surge forward.

Petal surfaced at the far end and tipped her head back under the small waterfall, where the water rushed over a lip of rock before slowing and spreading into the wide pool, the surface marked with raindrops.

Allie took off her dress and jum₁ᵣ
The chill of the water took the day's heaι .
a second. She breathed out, sinking slowly, eyes ◟ ◟
to the greenish water. There was no earthly pull on her
body, just a slow drifting down, a stream of bubbles
trailing to the surface. She couldn't help picturing Mae
underwater, her hair waving in the harbour currents,
the shadow of the dinghy far above. Suddenly her heart
was pounding and there was no air left in her lungs and
she jabbed her feet deep into fine oozing silt to find the
bottom and push to the surface.

She looked around for Petal, who called, 'Come
over here. You can see the pointy mountain behind
Julia's place. Hermit's Bluff. Some guy lives up there in
a shack. Almost never comes into town. I can't get her
to admit it but someone told me that Julia has a thing
going with him.'

From where Allie floated on her back, her heart still
beating hard, the tree trunks seemed to lean over the
creek, tilting at precarious angles, crowding out the small
window of sky overhead. The light was fading and the
forest path they came along had disappeared into shadow.
She paddled over to Petal. 'Saul Philips was my mother's
first love.'

'Oh really?' Petal raised her eyebrows.

'So he lives at the end of the valley?'

'Yeah.'

'Where exactly? Tell me where he lives.'

'On his father's place… well, beyond his father's
house, further along the creek. In a little cabin.'

'And is he married?' He couldn't be. She had always
imagined him waiting too.

'No. Not married. At least not at the moment. I don't know people's history. I've only been here a little while.' She reached over and stroked Allie's shoulder underwater, 'Doesn't this water make your skin feel soft?' She touched her own arm, 'So is your mother coming up too?'

'No. I'm going back. She's at home, or will be soon.' She followed Petal up onto the big rock that was warm and slick with rain. Perhaps this was Mae's kissing rock.

Petal sat up and started plaiting her hair. 'You're an outsider until you've been here at least thirty years, or so everyone keeps telling me.'

'I was born here. Well, in town.'

'Yes, but you went away. So I don't know what that makes you. Julia would know about Saul, wouldn't she? Ask her. And tell me what you find out.'

'How old are you?'

'How old do you think?'

Allie shrugged, 'Twenty?'

'I'm the same age as Julia. Twenty-seven. She's like twenty-seven going on forty, don't you think? Sometimes she treats me like the naughty kid camping up in the forest.'

'You camp in the forest?'

'Didn't you know? I live up the back of Julia's property in my caravan. I parked it there a few years ago. Couldn't tow it out now, though, even if I still had a car. Julia's bloody trees have closed me in. The van will just disintegrate there I guess.' She finished her long braid and turned to Allie. 'Want me to plait yours?'

Allie turned her back to Petal and shut her eyes to the familiar sensation of fingers threading through her long hair, tugging painfully at her scalp.

Petal spoke close to her ear, 'What do you think someone who's lonely looks like?'

'Huh?'

'You said you thought Julia was lonely. How do you know?'

'Well... I don't know. She's on her own here and she wants me to stay.'

Petal took an elastic hair band from her wrist and tied the end of Allie's plait. 'I saw her shoot a calf once. Someone hit it out on the road in front of her place. She put the gun to its head and blew its brains out. Then she went home and had a cup of tea. She's tough as anything, you know. She doesn't need other people.'

Allie shrugged. Her skin smelt of the brackish creek water and the plait was too tight. She stood up and pulled her damp dress over her head.

The sugary smell of baking reached her as she walked through the misty rain and up the back steps. She stopped on the verandah to watch Petal crossing the paddock, picking her way through the shoulder-high trees. When Allie turned to open the glass door into the house, her legs turned to water at the sight of Julia sitting at the kitchen table, her face in her hands, slowly moving her head from side to side as if grinding her hands into her face. Allie sank down on the damp verandah boards and wrapped her arms around her legs.

Julia opened the door and came to sit close beside her. A stream of fruit bats flew over the house towards the forest and the smell of the lemon pie grew stronger. The longer Julia was silent, the more afraid Allie felt.

'Allie?' Her aunt's voice shook. 'They've found her. Mae's body. Around at Middle Harbour. I just got a phone call…'

'Who? Who said they'd found her?' Allie heard her own voice as if from a distance, while her eyes followed the drips falling from her plait onto the boards, where the water sat in neat circles, like plump drops of blood.

'The policeman left his number,' Julia put her hand on Allie's arm. 'In case you want to speak to him. Come inside.'

She shrugged Julia's hand off. 'But she was the best swimmer.' Her voice was just a whisper, 'We swam in the harbour all the time.' The bats were still flying into the distance, as if nothing had changed.

Julia nodded. 'Yeah. She was a good swimmer. We'll have her… body sent up here. I said that we wanted her up here. I'll ring Barry Brooks in town. He did Mum and Dad's funerals.' She rubbed her face. 'Something happened didn't it, that last night? Before she went out? Did something happen?'

Allie slowly undid her plait. She had lain awake for hours after Tom came, waiting for the calm, waiting for him to go. She could have got up and stopped Mae going down to the harbour, she could have done something.

She let Julia reach an arm around her and, as she leaned into her aunt's body, she remembered the day that she and Mae had found a fairy penguin at Goat Island, its bloated body split open and leaking the salty stench of death. They had stood on the rocks looking down at it, its fur matted and dirty and its beak open in a grotesque yawn. Her stomach cramped and she doubled over, the terrible smell of the burning pie all around them.

chapter four

The rain gouged at the land and washed streams of red mud into the creeks. In the morning, Julia brought her tea and buttered toast in bed, then Allie followed her aunt down the paddock, where the girl slid the saplings from their pots and slowly packed soil around them, her fingers in the red dirt, pressing and pressing at the grains of soil while the rain beat down on her. She could still feel the last warm touch of Mae's skin on hers. The frantic hand waking her, to urge her down the stairs to tell Tom to leave. Her own fingers left watery muddy marks on her legs.

Julia gave her the job of pricking-out the tiny seedlings from the trays into individual tubes. 'Just don't damage the roots or stem,' she said as she demonstrated. 'If you do, then chuck it. Best to spend time growing only the strongest ones.'

Allie spent hours in the quiet of the potting shed, carefully lifting the little four-leafed plants, their delicate roots quivering. Even while it rained outside, the sprinklers sprayed mist onto the hairy leaves of the tiny trees. She sat on the damp wooden chair in the corner, the sweat rolling down her body, waiting for the seedlings to grow and watching the discarded ones wilt on the ground.

When they came up for Mae's father's funeral, her mother told her, 'This is just meat, you know.' She had pinched her arm. 'Bodies go back to dust but we leave traces here and there, atoms of ourselves. We float in the air everywhere we have ever been. Every word spoken, every breath exhaled. Every drop of sweat. My father and mother are still all around this farm.'

While Julia spread straw in the chicken house, Allie rested her cheek against the cool plaster walls of the bedroom and trailed her fingers along the stainless steel of the kitchen sink. She stood at the bathroom mirror, close, so her breath fogged the glass, while she searched for Mae in her own wide-set eyes and small nose. She hurried to her bedroom and pulled out the musty cotton sundresses that had hung in the wardrobe since Mae left. She tried them on one after another, dropping them to the floor. Green spots and blue flowers and light pink with blue piping. The thin material hung loosely, her small breasts lost in the bodice. Through the fabric, she cupped the rounded shape of her breasts, her hands warm and tender, the same way that the First Love had touched Mae.

Outside, she lifted her face to the rain. This very drop may have once slid down Mae's cheek, the clouds trapped inside the valley walls year after year, the same drops of rain falling back into the valley. It was salty on her tongue, like tears, like blood, and for a moment she could taste her mother. Then there was nothing but the ceaseless rain, running down her body, soaking the soil, filling the creeks.

The First Love would hold the strongest traces of her mother. His skin would still carry her touch. Their afternoons by the creek must be held somewhere in his body.

Allie went inside and put on one of her mother's dresses, looping the belt tight. She walked down the muddy driveway and along the gravel road that followed the curves of the meandering creek. She would walk until she found him.

A car came around the corner and she stepped off the road into the dense bush, sinking deep into the dark leaf litter as she gripped the slippery tree trunks and vines and pulled herself up the steep hill. The soaking rain entered her nose and eyes and glued her stringy hair to her cheeks. Everything was wet, and as she climbed, she surrendered herself to the blood-warm air and rain.

She found a forestry road cutting a clay swathe through the trees and then narrow animal tracks that led through a wall of prickly lantana to an abandoned banana plantation. The banana palms leaned down the hill, small overripe fruit hanging in heavy bunches and purple flowers dripping pollen. She pressed her cheek hard against a shining rain-slick trunk, like Mae would when they hid in the Botanic Gardens at night. In the dark, after the park rangers had gone, Mae would run across the springy grass to one of the huge fig trees and climb its buttress roots. Later, Allie would lean back against her mother, wrapped in the coat that Mae turned fur-side in, and she would reach up to trace the indentations that the tree had left on her mother's cheek.

Through the tattered banana leaves she could see down to the emerald green paddocks dotted with tin roofs. If she were Mae, she would know which was his. Mae would walk down the hill and straight into his waiting house.

The last letterbox at the end of the valley had 'Philips' painted across it in uneven black letters. Saul Philips. The dogs started barking before she had reached the first bend in the driveway so she slipped into the bush and slowly approached the white weatherboard house with its neat mown lawn and dripping Hills Hoist. The dogs strained at the end of their chains, tails and hackles stiff, and a peacock with a drooping tail peered down at her from the roof of a tin shed.

A woman with short grey hair came out onto the verandah and called the dogs back to their kennel. She reached up to a shirt hanging on the line strung under the verandah roof and pressed it to her cheek before slowly unpegging the clothes and folding them onto a chair.

Allie backed away through the bushes and found a well-worn path leading around the base of a steep rocky bluff. It led her over a small side creek where she stepped from boulder to boulder, the water tumbling under her, reeds pulled straight by the current.

The timber cabin was in the middle of a small clearing, its wood dark with rain, the roof a patchwork of second-hand tin. She moved quietly through the bush at the edge of the clearing and squatted in under a tangle of lantana near the house. Hanging from the verandah beam were his wire shapes. A dog with nails for teeth, a unicorn, and faces, turning slowly in the breeze, dripping with rain. There was a pair of his muddy leather boots by the door and a haphazard stack of firewood. She settled in the damp gloom under the lantana and waited for him to show himself to her.

Finally, in the fading light, after what seemed like hours, she walked up the wooden stairs and went straight to the wire face hanging from the corner of the verandah. She stroked the thin strips of metal curling into cupid's bow lips and long wild hair. They were her mother's almond-shaped eyes. My eyes, she thought and caressed the hard grey wire. She unhooked it from the nail and hurried across the lawn.

Of course it was her mother. All the face needed was the crooked eye tooth that Allie and Mae shared. 'Our vampire tooth,' Mae used to call it. Mae would let her sleep in the big bed on the nights that Tom didn't come and before she turned off the light, she reached for Allie, 'Good night, little vampire.' Allie would arch her neck for her mother to press the tooth into her skin. 'You're marked now.' Mae pushed her cool finger into the faint mark her tooth left. 'You're mine.'

If Tom went in the middle of the night, Allie would wake in her downstairs bed to the sound of his car engine booming around the narrow street and she would wait for Mae to come down and collect her. When she was little, Mae used to carry her up the stairs, her sleepy limbs knocking the banister and brushing against the cool plaster wall. The sheets smelt of cigarettes, perfume and sweat and her mother's naked body was warm and soft.

In the mornings, she watched Mae's pale sleeping face and looked for the flicker of a pulse at her neck, a sign that the heart was still urging the blood around her mother's body. She wondered how much blood vampires needed. A bowlful? Or just the puddle under the raw hunk of meat waiting to be cooked for the Sunday roast?

Sometimes Mae cooked Tom a roast with potatoes and carrots and onions, like she said her own mother and grandmother used to. While she carved, she would tell them how every Sunday her family went to eat with her grandparents and four uncles, all of them around the long dining table that her Pa built from a huge red cedar tree, the whole tabletop one piece of wood. They would arrive back from church to the smell of the slow-cooking lamb, a rich, sweet smell, the house hot from the wood stove that burned even in summer. Mae helped set the long table with a white tablecloth and was sent out to pick mint for the mint sauce, while her mother stirred the gravy, an apron over her good Sunday dress. The uncles watched Mae from the verandah, and flapped their white shirtfronts at the breeze before coming to sit at the table, all of them in a row along one side.

One day before Tom came to Sunday lunch, Allie found her mother crying on the steps of their tiny backyard, the smell of roasting meat strong in the air, an oven mitt dangling from her hands. 'We should have mint growing,' she wept. 'It's no good without mint sauce.'

Julia's room was quiet and dark when Allie left the house. The forest at night was even blacker than she had imagined. The bush pressed in on her and she stumbled on the narrow, rocky path. Small animals blundered away through the undergrowth and she listened for the feral dogs that Julia said ran in packs in the hills. She imagined them silently tracking her through the bush, muzzles lifted to catch her scent.

He was never home during the day. She had waited and waited in her place under the lantana but he didn't come. There had been signs of him—a window propped open and shirts strung on the verandah clothesline— but the house was always quiet, just the tin roof creaking in the heat and the currawongs crying out as they flew overhead.

She walked slowly across the clearing towards his open bedroom window, the lawn silvery with moonlight. The wire shapes hanging on the verandah moved in the darkness and an owl flew out of the forest, its wing-beats loud and close. She reached his window and leaned on the sill, the wood hard against her ribs. There he was at last, one arm stretching across the bed towards her, fingertips half-curled as if beckoning. She stood perfectly still, only her eyes moving, tracing the way his limbs had fallen in the night, following the arrow of dark hairs down to the sheet twisted around his waist. His face was turned away from her and she willed him to sigh and shift in his sleep and turn towards her so she could see his face, so she could recognise something of herself in him, some small sign. She imagined Mae sleeping beside him, her creamy body curved around his, their bellies rising and falling together. Allie sank to her knees in the damp grass under his window and matched her breath to his, the cool air streaming down her throat.

chapter five

Julia followed her niece at a distance, her torch lighting the unfamiliar narrow path through the forest. As they approached Little Banana Creek, she realised Allie was going to Saul's place and she stopped, her feet suddenly heavy, the same churning in her gut as when Mae used to run into the house and dump her school bag before slipping out the back door to meet him.

She continued over the creek and in the moonlight could see Allie standing at his window. She wanted to grab the girl away and shake her. Shake her then rock her. Rock her in her arms like her own mother used to do. Like she saw Saul do to Mae one day down by the river. She had hidden in the bushes and watched them, a kind of agony to see Mae's face shining under his touch.

An old helplessness that she hadn't felt in years rose in her and she rested her face into her hands and pressed her fingers hard onto her eyelids. She was no better than her father when he used to sneak around after Mae and Saul. She was no better than her father in lots of ways.

Since Allie had come to the farm, scraps of old memories had been rising in her. The yellow lace dress Mae was wearing the day she left, her hair pinned high as if she were going to a dance. Mae had run out into the rain, heaved her suitcase into the tray of the ute and settled the baby onto the passenger seat. 'Say goodbye to Mum,' she had said as she tucked the blankets around the baby's face. 'And will you tell Saul? Promise you'll tell him goodbye for me?' Her skin showed pink through the wet dress as she tied the tarp over her bags. 'Julia, will you tell him that I'm sorry? Hey, don't look so glum... it'll all be okay. You can come later and we'll live together, eh? You can help look after the baby.'

Julia remembered standing under the jacaranda tree looking down the driveway, long after the red tail-lights had disappeared, long after Mae would have reached town and the train station and left the ute there, keys in the ignition, long after she would have boarded the train and settled into a compartment and slid away into the night. Julia had waited outside for hours, a fluttering in her chest like a panicked bird.

Allie was walking back across the clearing towards her, Saul's house still dark behind her. Julia tried to think of what she should say but she knew she had little of her mother's sensitivity. She was blunt like her father. Blunted.

She waited for Allie to see her where she sat beside the path, but the girl passed by, just an arm's length away and disappeared into the dark of the forest. Anyway, this was not the right day. Julia leaned back against a tree and tried not to think of the Hanley brothers waking soon and, after their breakfast, walking over to the cemetery to dig Mae's grave. The ropes that they slung under the coffins always slipped so smoothly through their solid hands. She sat for a long time, looking up at the comforting shapes of the tall trees, imagining their roots slowly spreading through the whole valley again, laying a vast web of underground life. She used to spend hours lying on the forest floor, listening to the birds and the wind in the leaves. Sometimes she would drift to sleep and wake with a start, late for the afternoon milking. That was how Neal had found her. He told her that he watched her sleeping for a couple of hours, the dappled light moving across her face as the sun dropped.

She looked over to Saul's place, he'd be getting up soon to milk at his father's dairy. He had touched her once, when she was thirteen, down at the cattle dip. She had gone to tell him that Mae had left the valley and the instant that she told him, her head began to spin and he had dropped his hammer and knelt beside her. And there in the sun by the dip, he had stroked her, his big hand gently cradling her head and even then she knew that it was Mae he was touching.

She got back to her farm just as the sun was rising, the bottom of her jeans wet and muddy. Down at the old dairy, she had to clear dirt away to drag open the heavy wooden door and let the first light into the musty shed. A bale of hay had broken apart and was turning to dust on the floor, and along the corner beam, little black bats were settling for their day's sleep. They shuffled their wings and tried to protect their twisted faces from

the daylight. She sat heavily on a dusty wooden bench
and thought again of Saul's touch that day down at the
cattle dip and how she had missed her one chance to
tell him that Mae had said goodbye.

chapter six

The day of the funeral was a high blue-sky day like the morning Mae disappeared. A silent jet left a wisp of vapour in the cloudless sky. Allie walked beside Julia up the path to the small wooden church, past the bushes steaming in the sun. She wanted the clouds and rain to descend again and slowly wrap the trees and buildings in mist.

She sat beside Julia in the front pew, in one of Mae's old dresses, soft blue cotton with puffed sleeves. Her eyes blinked slowly and her blood moved like syrup in her veins. Sounds sagged through the air, the whispering and shuffling of feet, the walls creaking in the morning sun and the organist's sheet music fluttering to the polished floor.

Julia reached out to finger the fabric of Allie's dress and whispered, 'That was one of her favourites. I'm surprised she didn't take it with her.' She smoothed the cotton onto Allie's thigh.

Allie looked down at Julia's hand, the thick knuckles and red dirt under the fingernails. Julia's hand and her own leg. Solid, warm flesh, blood moving through their veins. She kept her eyes down, away from the coffin at the front of the church. In the blue of her dress she saw the ocean carrying the little Islander girl far out to sea, cradling her sleeping form.

She turned to look for him again in the rows of faces. Of course she would recognise him, she had seen the pale outline of his body in the dark and heard his breath easing in and out. When she got home from his house that morning, she had sat up on her bed watching the sunrise, every brighter wash of light bringing the moment of the funeral closer.

'Mae Curran was a daughter of this community and we hold our children dear.' The minister was fat, sweat shining on his pale moon face. 'It's fitting that she should come home to rest in the bosom of her family and community.'

From the corner of her eye she could see sun reflecting off the white lacquered coffin. Mae would hate the gold handles on the coffin, such shiny gold. Cheap and tacky, she would think. Allie remembered what Mae said about the trail of atoms that people left behind and imagined them leaking from the coffin, spreading up the red-carpeted aisle and through the double wooden doors. Her mouth suddenly flooded with saliva, and she felt nausea swell at the back of her throat and nose. She fixed her eyes on the minister's hands, his white fingers resting like slugs on the lectern.

'Let us carry her in our hearts and celebrate her life. Please rise for the hymn.'

How her mother would hate the gold handles. Allie knew every single thing that Mae hated. Lukewarm tea, prickly woollen blankets and the way Tom left golden drops of piss on the toilet seat.

She and Julia stood beside the minister at the bottom of the church steps as people filed past, sighing, murmuring. Old women in net hats, waving paper fans at their shiny faces, tight black suits stretched over farmers' backs and plump women with wet-mouthed babies. Where was the First Love? Sweat trickled down her back, and a sudden breath of breeze made it a cool line on her skin.

An old woman took Allie's arms, squeezing them tightly with gnarled fingers. 'My goodness, you're a little Mae,' she smiled. The woman's perfume was too sweet and orange face powder had marked the collar of her dress. 'It's just lovely to see you again my dear, but so sad that you come home to us for this.' She had tears in her eyes. 'It breaks my heart to bury my Mae. A day of heartbreak for us both. The number of funerals I have been to at this church, I can't count. Too many. Altogether too many.' She let go of Allie's arms. 'It's a terrible thing to lose your mother.' She turned to Julia, 'In case we don't get a chance to talk at the hall later, I'd like to see Allie soon. This week. Please telephone Dan or myself to arrange it, dear.'

As the old woman followed the line of people wandering down the path to the graveyard, Julia leaned over and whispered, 'Your great-grandmother.' Allie nodded, 'Yes. I remember.' And she watched the old woman pass through the gate and walk towards a pile of red dirt.

Beside Allie, the minister kept wiping his palms and

face with a big white handkerchief. He smiled then fished a second hanky from his back pocket and offered her the ironed square. She pressed it to her nose, it had the smell of tea towels and sheets from the linen closet at home.

Julia touched her shoulder. 'Allie? This is Saul.'

He was right in front of her, smiling, his eyes crinkling just like Mae had said. But he was too short. Mae had reached her hand up and shown her how tall he was, way above Mae's head, but this man was not much taller than Allie. And his skin was more tanned than she had imagined, stretched over high cheekbones.

Julia stepped too close. 'She's been wanting to meet you, Saul. She's been asking about you.'

He squeezed her hand as he spoke, 'I'm so sorry about your mother. Really sorry.' She looked down at the dark hairs coiling on his forearm and on the back of his broad hand.

Her voice was barely a whisper. 'Didn't you know we were waiting for you to come and find us?' The hot air scoured her throat.

'What?' he bent towards her, his brow furrowed. 'Say that again.'

She could smell him, salty sweat and something else. His cheek was close to her, blue-black dots of whisker and the soft fleshy curl of his ear. This was what Mae had known, this warm touch of his hand. She knew she should say something else, that she should let go of his hand, his calluses hard against her palm.

The minister leaned over. 'Nice to see you, Saul.'

She wanted him to lead her away from Julia and the minister, away from everyone waiting to bury her mother.

He slipped his hand from hers and smiled.

The dirt was too loud on the coffin. Allie watched Julia lean out over the grave to drop a handful onto the shiny white, her dress straining at the armpits. Red earth exploding on the white. Clay had smeared the lid where it bumped against the side of the grave on the way down and she could hear the wood of the coffin quietly creaking in the hot sun. A rustling came from the mound of dirt beside the grave. It wanted to return to the earth, to layer itself heavy on the coffin.

The minister spoke again and his words were just noise rising with the shimmering heat and the scent of wet earth.

Then it was over and the people started moving away, eager to leave the ugly gaping hole in the ground.

Julia turned to her, brushing the red soil from her fingers. 'There's a tea over in the hall now. I'd better put in an appearance. Are you coming?'

Allie shook her head.

'You want to stay here on your own for a while?'

She nodded.

Julia hesitated then walked over the grass towards the yellow wooden hall sitting high on its brick piers, her long hair loose and shining in the bright sun.

The man with the shovel was talking to a red-faced farmer in a suit and wide-brimmed felt hat. Every so often the man eyed the grave and shifted his feet. He couldn't start filling it in if Allie was still there. She sat on a cool stone grave and looked down at her muddy shoes. She wanted to take them off and let the red mud ooze between her toes. As long as she was there, the dirt wouldn't go into the grave.

After her grandfather's funeral, she and Mae had sat under a tree in that same graveyard while everyone had tea and scones in the hall. Mae had lain back on the grass and slept, and Allie waved the flies away from her until Julia came looking for them and drove them back to the farm.

'Allie?' It was Saul. He sat down beside her, and rested his arms on his knees. 'How are you holding up? It's tough going, I know.'

She watched his fingers playing with a blade of grass. He had square-tipped fingers like hers.

'My mum is buried in here too. Over there.' He pointed to a shady corner of the graveyard. Suddenly he reached an arm around her and squeezed her shoulder. Her heart started to race, heat rising through her at the weight of his arm around her.

'When I was at high school, I used to come in once or twice a week, just to sit under the trees, in the quiet.' He paused. 'Your mum used to come with me.'

'Just the two of you?'

'Yeah.' He dropped his arm. 'The whole community ends up here. My dad's already paid for his plot.' He looked around and nodded towards the pile of dirt at Mae's grave. 'Your mum's parents are just over there. And one of her uncles and her grandfather and at least one cousin that I know of.'

'I know about the first kiss.'

'The first kiss?' he raised his eyebrows.

She watched his lips forming the words and wanted to reach out to press against their soft cushion and make them yield that kiss. 'You and my mum.'

'Oh,' he smiled. 'She talked to you about that?'

'Yeah. All the time.'

'She did?'

She nodded. She could see herself reflected in his black pupils.

He smiled. 'I remember that kiss. It was very innocent.' He leaned back and rested his elbows on the grave. 'Afterwards she led me up to one of her father's cows and sprayed milk into my mouth.' He looked over his shoulder. 'Whose grave are we on? Bertha Mason. The Masons aren't here today, so it won't matter.'

'Why did you fall out of love with her?'

'Is that what she told you? That I fell out of love with her?'

'Isn't that what happened?'

He looked past her. 'It's not how I'd describe it.'

'So what happened?'

'Oooh, it was pretty complicated there at the end.'

'Do you mean the balloon man?'

He grimaced. 'Yeah, I mean the balloon man. The hot-air balloon man.'

She shook her head and waited for him to say something more.

He stood up and smiled. 'So, are you coming over to the hall?'

She followed him across the grass, watching the muscles of his back move under the faded red shirt. At the gate, she turned back to check on the gravedigger where he stood leaning on his shovel. Beyond him, the sky above the mountains was relentlessly clear, all the clouds vanished into the hard blue.

The hall was filling with people, talking, stirring sugar into their tea, reaching for sandwiches and slices of pound cake. Women in net hats stood behind trestle tables, pouring tea from big metal teapots and waving flies from the cake. They smiled at her, their eyes quickly sliding away.

Allie's great-grandmother was walking around with a big teapot, topping up teacups. 'Don't you want a cuppa, Allie my dear?'

'No, thank you.'

The old woman put the teapot down on a table and lifted the lid. She shook her head. 'They made it too strong.' She pulled a bobby pin from her hair and adjusted her small hat. 'It's lovely you're back in the valley, dear. We're all so glad you're back. You have lots of family here, you know.' She waved her hand around the room at the people standing in small groups, talking, laughing, patting their mouths with paper serviettes.

She fitted the lid back onto the teapot with a sigh, 'Oh well, things don't always turn out like you think. I'm going to have you down for lunch in the next couple of days and we can talk properly. Julia and I will arrange it. The ladies over there have cordial too, if you'd like it, dear.' She walked away carrying the teapot before her.

'Here you are, lassie. Take one of these.' A man in a grey suit offered her sandwiches on a small white plate.

She took a neat triangle of bread but held it tipped away from her so she wouldn't see the glistening lumps of egg filling.

'I'm sorry about your mum, love,' the man said. He looked her up and down, his eyes pausing at her breasts for a moment. 'Lucky you've got Julia, eh? She's a good lady.' He nodded and took a sip of his tea. 'I was a friend of your grandfather's. We set up the meat pool together. He knew lots about slaughtering, he grew up on a beef farm you know. He always promised to take me out west to show me his dad's old farm, and to do some pig shooting but we never got there.'

Julia appeared at her side, sweat staining her dress dark under the arms and at the tight creased waistband. 'Hello.' She leaned close to Allie, 'Let me show you something. Excuse us Roy.'

They walked to the open window at the far end of the hall, passing Saul where he leaned against the wall, under the portrait of the Queen. He held his teacup under his nose, inhaling the steam while he listened to the small talk of a woman with a baby on her hip. When Allie had mentioned the balloon man, he had smiled a funny twisted smile, as if he wasn't sure what to say. Allie wanted to go over and interrupt his conversation and tell him that she had always known which stories Mae meant her to believe.

Julia brushed the crumbs from her plate out the window. 'So you met Saul at last.'

'Yeah.'

'What were you talking about over in the graveyard?'

'Nothing. What do you want to show me?'

'Nothing.' Julia looked closely at her. 'Have you eaten anything?'

'I'm not hungry.'

'You know, if you go walking at night, take a torch for the snakes.'

'What?'

She looked directly at Allie, 'Take a torch next time. They're on the shelf near the back door. Snakes are out at night, you know. It's not the best time to go wandering around the valley.'

'She walked around at night.'

'I know. She took a torch. Are you going to eat that sandwich?'

Allie shrugged and passed it to her aunt, who tossed it out the open window onto the neatly mown grass, where it lay, its yellow guts exposed.

Julia turned to her and smiled. 'It's all right. They expect me to do things like that.'

Outside the hall, the whirring of cicadas was piercing. An old dog slunk under the wooden building and disappeared into the darkness. Allie followed him, sliding between the lattice into the dim forest of shadowy brick piers, footsteps loud above her, high-heeled shoes marching across the floorboards.

She looked out between the piers to the bright white sunlight. On the other side of the road, two little girls in their swimmers were squealing, running back and forth through a sprinkler. Down at the motel by the beach, Mae had rubbed cream into Allie's sunburnt skin before Allie lay back on the stiff sheets and listened to Mae and Tom argue on the verandah outside, her hot skin prickling.

The dog came and sniffed her and turned in a circle before settling, panting, onto the cool earth. So Julia knew she had left the house last night. She didn't care what Julia knew. She wished she had woken Saul, called his name through the window like Mae would have and pulled herself over the sill to lie down beside him.

A group of people walked along the path beside her, just their legs showing. They crossed the lawn to the shade of the big camphor laurel tree. Through the lattice she could see that he was with them, smiling, lighting someone's cigarette. She used to lie in her bed, imagining him coming for them. Even when she was little, she would listen to the cars on the street outside and the hollow sound of the train crossing the Harbour Bridge, and think of him going from house to house, tracking them down. One day there would be a knock and there he would be in the doorway.

Petal squatted on the cement path and looked through the lattice. 'Hi.' She ducked underneath and crawled across the dirt, marking her white lace skirt. 'Thank God it's a bit cooler under here.' She passed Allie a glass of red cordial and opened a silver cigarette case. 'Julia's up there, determined to piss them all off.' The fragrant smoke from Petal's clove cigarette merged with the smell of buttery sausage rolls and hot grass. 'I tell her that she takes them for granted. If she really needed them, they'd be there for her, you know. She doesn't give them a chance.' She rested back on her elbows and blew smoke rings. 'What are you looking at, darl?'

'Him.'

'Saul?'

'Mmmm.'

Petal smiled and shook her head. 'Oh yeah. Imagine him at seventeen.'

Silently, they watched him. He leaned against the tree, listening to the people around him, his hand stroking the bark on the tree trunk. Then he turned and seemed to be looking straight at them, a half-smile on his face.

Petal whispered, 'Don't worry, he can't see us through the lattice. It's too dark under here.'

Allie took a sip of the drink and the intense sweetness caught in her throat. She was suddenly desperate to remember the details of Mae's face but couldn't conjure even the shape of her mother's nose or the way her dimples flashed when she smiled. Allie's gorge rose and she felt she might just lean over and spew her bloodied insides onto the grey dirt. She shoved the glass back at Petal, spilling some of the drink onto the ground. Petal took the glass and drank it, then stubbed her cigarette out. 'Julia wants to go. Are you ready?'

chapter seven

He woke before the alarm clock and lay in the dark, his mind still numb with sleep, for a moment not understanding the sound of his dog's claws clicking on the wooden floor. He rolled over, tucking the sheet around him, and suddenly recalled the sight of Mae's coffin slipping down into the grave. He couldn't imagine her body contained within that white box, her strong limbs stilled. They used to run down the hill to the creek together, the blanket stretched between them and flapping like a great wing in the humid air. There was the sound of their feet on the spongy pasture and the rumble of a distant tractor and there was Mae, her hair streaming behind her as they flew down the hill.

He got out of bed and pulled on his jeans and T-shirt in the dark. At the kitchen sink, he stood looking out at the faint line of light above the trees and ate a slice of his stepmother's orange cake.

It was years since he had thought of how Mae used

to lie naked on the blanket for him, pale against the dark wool. She would let him put his lips to her soft breasts, to her moist neck, to the palm of her hand, to her stomach. He had sucked her skin into him, taken her soft flesh into his own. He had cupped that belly in his hands, kissed it, blessed it, unknowing.

He pulled on his boots and stepped out into the half-light. He knew every turn and rise in the path he had cut to his father's house. At the dairy, he walked slowly through the gathering cows, their big warm bodies swaying heavily out of his way.

'Hi Dad,' he called.

'Son. How'd you sleep?' His father limped across the shed and let another cow into a stall.

They worked in silence, the rhythmic sound of the milking machine filling the room. When they finished, they stood in the doorway and looked out at the soft morning light.

His father knocked a clod of mud from his boot. 'Isn't the girl the spitting image of her mother? Clarry had told me, but still, I was surprised. God, she used to really unwire your brain, that Mae. I remember how you used to be.'

'Is that so?' It had taken him a moment to recover every time he caught sight of the girl sitting at the front of the church. She had the same long dark hair and wide mouth as Mae, even the precise curve of cheek.

His father laughed. 'She gave you such a hard time. I just hope the daughter's not too much like her mother.'

'What do you mean?'

'You know… you wouldn't want the girl to do to some boy what her mother did to you. I imagine folks will be watching for it. I know they will be.'

'Since when are you so up on the valley gossip?' He shook his head, and his voice rose, 'You know, what she did is my business. Mine and hers. Nothing to do with you, Dad, and nothing to do with the girl.'

'Yeah? Well, you forget that I was there,' his father snorted and walked down to the house.

Saul leaned back against the wall of the dairy, surprised at the heat of his old shame. He had just turned sixteen when his father had stopped him, there in the yard, at the same time of day, as they started to walk back to the house for breakfast.

'I've been waiting for you to say something to me. But…' His father had shaken his head. 'You're an idiot. You're a bloody idiot, you know. It's obvious to the whole valley that she's carrying!'

'What?' Saul, wary of his father's raised hand, hadn't understood.

'What do you think you were doing, then? Why the hell didn't you take precautions? What kind of fool are you?'

'What? Who's carrying… ?' Then an icy chill had trickled into Saul's body and he knew what his father meant. He saw it. How her dress had caught on the small mound of her stomach down at the creek the day before, how the fabric shifted over it. Her taut breasts under his tongue.

'Who's carrying?' his father laughed and shook his head incredulously. 'Are you serious? I thought you were smarter than that Saul. A lot bloody smarter.'

Somehow he had found himself swinging at his father, who was strangely soft and yielding. His fists

disappeared somewhere into his father's body, then the
two of them were on the ground, wrestling, and he
heard a voice, high and whining, 'But we never did it.
Mae, oh Mae, oh Mae.' His fist hit the ground over and
over, skin and bone jarring on the compacted dirt, then
his father was gone and Saul was left lying on the ground
by the shed, his eyes wide to the clear morning sky.

In the afternoon he had waited for her in the shade
of the mango tree. She came through the gate flushed
with heat, her smile fading when she saw him. 'What
happened to your face?'

He turned and ran down the hill, the air around
him vibrating with the sound of cicadas, and as he ran
he tried to forget, for a moment, what his father had
told him.

At the creek she came to stand in front of him, all
shining hair and school dress, and took his hands. 'What
happened, Saul?'

'I had a fist-fight with my father.' He looked down
at their hands and then to the cotton dress over her
belly. He spat out the words, 'Were you just going to
wait until I figured it out? Why did I have to hear it
from my father, like some cheap valley gossip? How
could you let me be the last to know?'

When she spoke he could barely hear her over the
creek. 'I love you. I love you, Saul.' Those words that
he had waited to hear, that he had whispered in her
name, holding his hand over his mouth to take them
back into himself. 'It was... someone... at the Show.
Just someone at the Show, I'm so sorry.'

'Who?'

She shut her eyes and whispered, he had to lean

close to hear, 'A showman, the man who took people up in his hot-air balloon… remember you were away in Brisbane…'

The balloon man. One of those men who go around with the fairs, one of those hard-faced men. While Saul had been in Brisbane at his uncle's funeral, Mae had spread her legs for another man.

'How could you? How could you give some… stranger what you promised me?' He gripped her shoulders and pressed his mouth hard onto hers. There was the familiar slide of their lips together and breath ragged into each other's mouth. And then he was pulling her down onto the ground. He could go there too, like the dirty balloon man. The heat ran through him, snaking to his groin. He felt her firm belly under him as he fumbled with his fly and pulled at her underpants.

Then he looked down at her. Her eyes were shut and she was slowly shaking her head from side to side, grass in her hair and tears sliding down her cheeks. And all he wanted was to cradle her to him, to feel her skin sliding over her fragile bones and the press of her breasts against his chest. He levered himself off and knelt on the grass, his body trembling.

She got up, brushed the grass from her clothes and walked away, that body he knew so well, her golden legs moving under her school dress and her long dark hair down her back. He called after her, but knew she was too far away to hear, 'I hate you Mae. Do you hear me? I hate you for this.' He wanted to punch the balloon man. He wanted his fist to break on the bones of the man's face. Then she was gone and he was alone by the creek, his belt undone, his cock shrivelling and he thought the sound of the water would send him mad.

That night he had carried his mattress out into the garden and stretched naked and sweating under an old mosquito net tied to a branch. He woke to the raindrops stroking his cheek like gentle fingers and lay listening to the drops tapping on leaves until the water collected in his navel and the corners of his eyes. He got up and jogged across the grass with the mattress balanced on his head and sat on the verandah in the dark, listening to the rain and waiting for his father.

A light went on inside and there were footsteps through the house. Every morning since he could remember, he had woken to his father silhouetted in the golden light from the kitchen, a big broad-shouldered shape filling his bedroom doorway.

His father pushed open the screen door onto the verandah. 'Been raining long?'

He shook his head and stood up, avoiding his father's eyes. They walked down to the dairy in silence, the dog at their heels, his father shining a torch for snakes on the path. While his father started the milking machine, Saul walked slowly around the dark paddock, letting the dog bring in the last sleepy cows. In their stalls, the cows nosed the barley, their udders hanging full and tight. His father passed him a sterilised bucket and he walked up to the end stall to milk by hand the one cow frightened by the machine. Neither man mentioned Mae nor the darkening bruise on Saul's face but he couldn't help thinking about her, about where she would be moment by moment, helping her own father with the milking. He leaned his forehead against the cow's warm flank and tugged at the leathery udder, shooting stream after stream of milk into the foaming bucket. He tried to set his mind on the rhythm of the milking, but still she came to him, and finally he let himself picture her long slim hands on the cow's teats, her smile as she turned to look at him and spray the warm milk up into his mouth. He remembered her cool wet lips slipping under his and the resistance of her breast against his palm. His hands loosed from the cow and he pressed his face into its side to muffle the sound that came from him.

chapter eight

She dreamt that Mae was rowing them up the harbour,
oars splashing the oily water, the small dinghy weaving
its way into the darkness, the tide slowly drawing them
towards the Heads. Allie was sitting on the wooden
plank seat, looking back to shore, her fear growing with
every stroke. Then the drumming on the roof woke her
from the dream and she lay, her eyes wide open to the
dark, the sound of the rain pressing her down into the
mattress. Even though it took hours, Mae loved to row
way out towards the mouth of the harbour where the
swell was highest and the black water heaved under their
little boat. Mae would slither from her clothes and into
the water, her skin gleaming in the faint moonlight.
Like a slippery fish, she would dive under the dinghy,
bumping against it, her pale form blurry underwater.

'Come in sweetheart, come in with me,' she would
call up to where Allie sat clutching the tin sides of the
dinghy. Allie knew there were sharks gliding out there,

the faint splashes she could hear, their fins slicing the surface.

'Silly. They have nets out there to stop the sharks.' Mae bobbed up and down and waved her arm towards the lights at the harbour entrance. 'They have nets. Come on. Be adventurous, Allie. It's a midnight swim.'

The last time they went out together, Allie finally slid into the briny water, fear speeding through her as she swam to her mother. Their limbs glided together like warm silk and she clung to Mae's strong body as the swell lifted them then rolled away into the darkness. Mae pulled away from her and dove straight down, her white feet the last to slip under. Allie felt strangely peaceful, floating alone in the middle of the harbour with nothing but the glinting waves and the small dinghy. In the distance a ferry rumbled its way back to the Quay, its lights spilling onto the dark water. She had no doubt that Mae would reappear, breathless and exultant.

'It's like flying!' her mother cried as she burst to the surface. 'Swimming underwater is like gliding through the air, your hair streaming back, the world way below.'

Waves came from the darkness and jostled them. 'How deep is it here, Mum?'

'Deep.'

'How deep?'

'Oh…' Mae floated on her back, dark nipples pointed, 'maybe a mile or two deep.'

Allie clawed her way through the water to the flimsy dinghy, the depths pulling at her frantic legs.

❧

The rain was singing in the downpipes and falling in thick cords from the gutters. As the weak dawn light entered the house, Allie went to the back door and stood looking out. The dirt would be heavy on Mae's coffin now, the rain percolating down through the mud to make a sticky red seal on the lacquered wood.

She walked down the back steps and into the forest. Her dress was soon pasted to her thighs and the rain ran in runnels between her breasts and down the back of her neck.

As she entered Saul's clearing, a group of black-faced wallabies thumped a warning with their back feet and bounded away into the gloom of the forest.

Through the window she could see that his bed was empty, the sheet crumpled to one side. On the verandah table there was an empty coffee mug and a shirt hanging over the back of a chair. She touched her wet hand to the soft cotton of the shirt. She wanted to see the curl of his ear again and the way the corners of his mouth pulled down for a moment before he smiled.

'Is that you Allie?' He was behind her, at the foot of the stairs in a hooded yellow raincoat, his hand lifted to shield his face from the rain. 'What are you doing here?'

She took a step towards him.

He looked at the shirt in her hand. 'It's early to be paying a visit. I've only just finished milking.'

'I was just walking. Mum told me about the paths that you and she had.'

'Oh. A lot of them are overgrown now.' He started up the stairs, 'Would you like a cup of tea?'

'Okay.'

'Just go in,' he gestured towards the door as he hung his raincoat on a hook. 'It's not locked.' He followed close behind her as she walked inside. 'So, how are you coping with the rain? It's been pretty full-on, even for this time of the year.'

At last she was inside his house, in the dim spicy atmosphere, a row of plants along the windowsill, a glowing red leadlight window and a forest of wire sculptures hanging on twine from the high-pitched ceiling.

He struck a match and lit the gas stove. 'It's the wettest it's been in years. It's a real early wet this year. My dad reckons we're heading for one of the big floods.'

'I don't mind the rain,' she said. She wanted to explain that the rain, falling day after day, had come to soothe and contain her, that the clouds resting on the steep valley walls held her fast. She made her voice stronger. 'I do… I like the rain, now.'

'Like your mother.' He passed her a towel from a pile of folded washing.

She sat on a chair and pressed her face into the rough towel. Like Mae, she knew the smell of him and the way he slept, his body flung down onto the mattress, the tender white skin of his inner arm exposed.

'How did you sleep last night?' He stood at the kitchen bench and spooned tea-leaves into the pot.

'I think I heard a baby crying in the night.' She had lain awake for hours listening to the faint mewling outside, afraid of what she might find if she went to look for it.

He paused as he poured boiling water into the teapot then looked at her. 'Might have been a plover. They squawk around in the night.'

'A plover.'

'Or foxes. They can make strange noises. You know, I was surprised that Mae told you about the first time we kissed.'

'Why? Why wouldn't she tell me?'

'Milk?' He held up a big glass jug of milk, a layer of yellow cream on the top.

'Yes, please.'

'Come out onto the verandah.' He carried the tray of tea things. 'I guess I didn't imagine she would even think about it…'

'She told me lots, like how you danced with her that first time up at the hall, how she felt the muscles of your back under your shirt and how you smelt like soap.' She spoke slowly, watching the smile flicker at the corners of his mouth. She could read him just like she could read Mae.

He nodded. 'She left early, I remember. Her Dad came to pick her up and she was wearing a green dress with no sleeves.' He smiled and touched his upper arm, 'I could just see under her arms and the wisps of hair there. Her mum wouldn't let her shave.' His dog ran out of the bushes and up the steps to flop at his feet, its coat wet and sticky with grass seeds. 'Does it help to talk about her? I used to want to talk about Mum but Dad just couldn't do it. It was too hard for him.'

He passed her a cup of tea, his fingers big on the delicate saucer. Fingers that had touched the warm flesh of Mae's pregnant belly, only a thin sheath of skin between him and Allie's curled body.

She inhaled the steam from her cup. 'What did it feel like, her stomach, when she was pregnant?'

'Oh…' He paused. 'Firm… and kind of hard.'

'So you touched it?'

'Yeah.'

'Was she happy to be having me?'

'Was she happy? Oh yes. Yes, she was happy.' He smiled at her then rubbed a foot across his dog's belly and looked out to the forest where the misty clouds moved down the valley, snagging on the tallest trees.

Allie wanted all his memories of Mae. She wanted to know her mother paddling in the waterhole during a storm, her bright face floating above the rain-pocked water, limbs trailing greenly behind her. She wanted to see red mud squeezing between Mae's toes down by the creek, where she first took his hand under her school dress and held it against the swell of her breast.

She sat forward. 'Did you ever meet the balloon man? Did anyone actually meet him?'

'The balloon man again… yeah, he came to a few Shows. I met him.'

'You did?'

'Yeah.'

She was suddenly conscious of the way her wet dress stuck to her body and crossed her arms over her chest. 'Did you see them together?'

'No,' he shook his head. 'I was away… I didn't find out until later. She didn't tell me until quite a bit later.' He sat back in his chair and lifted his feet up onto a stool.

'But no-one saw them together, did they?'

He raised his eyebrows. 'What do you mean?'

She shrugged.

'People saw them together, Allie. Lots of people.'

When she was little she imagined the balloon floating

high above the crowd at the Showground, tethered to the ground with thick ropes, Mae and a dark-haired man held in the sway of the creaking wicker basket, the great canopy billowing above them and the town's streets laid out below, the river like a green ribbon tossed on the ground. For a while Mae used to talk about the balloon man a lot, but in that offhand kind of way that Allie had learned meant that she was just trying a story out. Then she simply stopped talking about him.

He put his tea down, with a slight frown. 'What gives you this idea that they weren't really together? Did she say something?'

'No. Not in so many words.' She watched his face carefully.

'So, what did she say?'

'That she went out with him for a little while.'

He nodded. 'Well, there you go.'

'But you were going out with her at the same time. She told me that, too.'

He looked at her a long moment. 'Well, I guess that's also right...'

She waited for him to say more. The rain suddenly stopped, leaving drifts of cool air and startled calls from birds in the forest. He was silent, looking down at his hands.

The weave of the cane chair was hard under her thighs and the tea bitter on her tongue. 'We were waiting for you to come and find us, you know.'

'That's what you said to me yesterday, isn't it?' He sighed. 'Was she really waiting for me?'

She nodded slowly.

His voice was quiet. 'When was this?'

'The whole time.'

'But did she say she was waiting for me?'

'She was waiting. We were both waiting.'

He was silent, then nodded. 'I'm sorry.'

She walked back through the forest thinking of Mae's stories and secrets, handfuls of them that Mae would sometimes let slip between her fingers. It was in the upstairs bed that her mother would lie back, her arms above her head, the stories slowly unfolding as she chose her words.

At the farmhouse Allie peeled off her wet clothes and dropped them to the bathroom floor. She lay back in the bath, her small breasts rising from the water, and she said his name out loud, letting it whisper around the bathroom, testing the sound of it. He had said he was sorry. She sank under the bath water and opened her eyes to the murky water, her hair silky around her face. Sorry for not coming to find them? Or sorry that he wouldn't say what they both knew to be true? It was up to him to offer it. He had to come to her like she had always imagined he would.

'Allie, are you in there?' The sound of Julia's footsteps through the house boomed underwater.

Allie surfaced. 'Yeah.'

'Are you having a bath?'

She slid back under the water. Julia had seen Mae and Saul together, she had been there, but Allie would never ask Julia what she knew. Allie wanted to keep them to herself.

Julia's muffled voice was close to the door, 'I'm cooking bacon and eggs for breakfast. Do you want some?'

Allie sat up, water sluicing from her. 'I want Saul to come to my birthday dinner.' Her voice echoed around the small room.

'Saul? Why Saul?'

'Can I ask him?'

There was a pause. 'Yeah. Sure.' Julia walked away from the door.

The bathwater was a reddish colour from the rusted water tank. As Allie dried herself she bent her knees to look between her legs. The blood would come soon, it should have come already. All the other girls in her class had started menstruating. She had seen her mother's blood, those mornings Mae woke and clattered down the stairs to the outside toilet, cupping her hands between her legs, leaving a dark stain blooming on the white sheet. And she had watched her mother throwing bloody pads into the incinerator, grey smoke threading through the branches of the big tree in the backyard. It was Allie's job to poke the pads with a stick until they were just powdery ashes.

Every day she looked for the blood between her legs and sometimes slid a finger inside herself, like she had seen her mother do. 'Just checking if it's started,' her mother used to say. Allie whispered her mother's words, 'Oh, nothing yet,' as she wrapped a towel around herself.

chapter nine

Julia was squatting on the verandah, sorting through her stacks of black plastic pots when Petal called from halfway up the driveway, 'There's a wallaby been hit, Julia. You'd better deal with it.'

Julia stood up slowly. She knew what to expect, a wide-eyed terrified animal, its useless legs scrabbling to get away. She walked to the shed and picked her rifle off the wall and two bullets from the box on the bench. 'How far up the road is it?'

Petal dropped a plastic bag of avocados onto the grass. 'You can have some of these if you like. It's right at the bottom of your driveway. I'll come back with you.'

The pale gravel road was bright with blood. The wallaby's lower half was contorted, its muscular back legs twisted the wrong way. As they approached, it grunted and frantically turned its narrow furry chest back and forth.

'Who hit it?' Allie had silently appeared at Julia's side, her bare feet muddy and dress wet.

'I don't know. Someone who didn't have the decency to stop.' Julia shifted the gun to her right hand and took a step towards the animal. It slumped down onto the road, its brown eyes following her every move. Its breath came in short panicked blasts and blood glistened on soft flared nostrils.

Then Allie was on her knees beside the wallaby, her small fingers tracing the length of the thick black tail. She stroked the wallaby's furry flank, dark with blood and silvery with droplets of light rain.

'I need to put it out of its misery Allie. You'll have to move back.'

'We can look after it.'

'Its back is broken. And probably its pelvis. See,' Julia pointed.

'Oh. So we'll kill it.'

'Yeah.'

Julia waited while Allie fingered the sticky blood where it soaked into the gravel. She suddenly saw that Allie was like her. More like her than Mae, who could never cope with dying animals or a cow birthing gone wrong.

Even as Julia loaded the rifle and stepped forward, the wallaby's body relaxed and the life passed from its eyes. A rush of urine diluted the blood spreading on the road.

Petal lit a cigarette. 'At least it had company as it died.'

Julia turned to her, surprised at the vehemence in her voice. 'You think we were a comfort to it, Petal? It's a wild animal. It died absolutely terrified. It would have been better off if we left it to die on its own.'

Petal shrugged and started up the driveway.

'Feel it,' said Allie, her hand on its bloated belly. 'It's still warm. It's dead but still warm.'

Julia squatted beside her niece and touched the soft pale fur of its belly. She wished she had come by herself and killed it straight away. It would be all over by now, the body already tossed into the bushes beside the road. She ran her fingers through the fur and found the fleshy pouch opening.

'What are you doing?' Allie sounded shocked, but leaned closer.

'Checking for babies. There are none. Let's get it off the road.'

Allie wouldn't move. Her eyes glistened with tears as she looked down at the dead animal. Julia wanted to sit on the muddy road beside the wallaby and take her niece into her arms but she knew if she did, her own tears would come. She rested her hand on Allie's shoulder, then reached down and gripped the wallaby's tail. She felt its vertebrae separating as she dragged it over the gravel and swung it into the tangled undergrowth.

chapter ten

Saul sat at his father's kitchen table and watched Iris wrap the lump of corned beef in a tea towel.

She nodded at him. 'Call your father again will you, Saul?'

His father was down at the dairy and from a distance, looked especially shrunken and frail. Saul leaned on the verandah railing and called, 'Dad! Dinner.' While he waited for his father to shut the heavy wooden gate and walk up to the house, he wondered again why Mae hadn't told Allie about his trip to Sydney and their argument in the milk bar. She had marched off down the road, her hair wild, the wriggling child in her arms. Allie in her arms. And he had gone back to his hotel and got drunk before catching the train south. When he had first got to Tasmania he would think of her every night, while he lay in his cold stone room at the back of the jeweller's workshop, the weight of the woollen blankets squeezing sensation from his limbs and the distance stretching achingly between him and Mae. On the weekends he spent hours chopping wood for the stove in the jeweller's workshop and for the fireplace in his room. Stripped to his damp steaming singlet in the stone courtyard, he swung the axe high like his father had taught him and let its weight drop and cleave the wood. He fed the fire in his room until it roared, then stripped to wash himself from a bucket. In the firelight he had looked down at his body, at the dark hair growing thicker on his chest and running down his stomach, around his pale penis. He had thought of Mae lying on the blanket by the creek, hands crossed over her breasts, smiling at him to come closer. The warm soapy water brought release but there was no joy in it, just an aching wave that broke into familiar emptiness.

'The bloody dairy pump has gone out again, Saul,' his father called as he walked across the yard. 'Will you have a look at it later?'

'Yep.'

His father reached the bottom of the steps and Saul turned to go inside. After a few minutes, his father came to the table as he always did, smelling of soap, his hair freshly combed back with water. When it was just the two of them, before Saul left for Tasmania, mealtimes were quiet, all their talking done out in the paddock while they worked. Now Iris kept them chatting through the whole meal, as if she were running a class on conversation skills.

She passed Saul the plate of buttered bread. 'I hear they've decided to put the highway right through the golf course. What about us! Where will we play?'

'Ah, it'll take them years to do anything.' His father

unfolded his serviette onto his lap.

'I'm just so mad that they can simply decide to do it. Oh, I feel all out of kilter after yesterday. I just hate burying young folk.'

'Don't talk to him about her. You'll end up in his bad books too.' His father looked over at Saul, smiling as he chewed.

'Don't be ridiculous, Dad.' Saul didn't smile back.

'Oh come on, you never wanted to hear the truth about her.'

Saul ignored his father. 'What do you know about how Mae died, Iris?'

She frowned. 'Just what you know, dear. That she drowned in the sea.'

'In the harbour,' he said.

His father reached for the mustard. 'Sydney Harbour. Sea. Same thing.'

'Did you ever see her swim, Dad?'

His father shook his head. 'Pass the white sauce, will you please, love. I'll finish it off. Where would I have ever seen her swim?'

Saul turned to Iris. 'I just thought you might have heard something. People are saying…'

His father licked the serving spoon. 'She always had a dozen stories circulating about her, that girl. She kept the valley gossips going.'

'What would people up here know, Saul?' said Iris. 'Huh? Remember when Sally Benson's girl went to Sydney and everyone was saying she'd become a prostitute? It wasn't true. Most of it's not true.'

'Ah, you couldn't be sure of anything with that girl, son. Nice enough lass, but she didn't tell it straight, eh?'

Saul put down his fork. 'What makes you such an expert on her?'

'Ah, this is all ancient history Saul.'

'You don't like to talk of those that are gone, do you Dad? You never mentioned Mum's name once after she died. It was as if she had never existed. I began to wonder if I was crazy, if I'd invented her.'

His father wiped his plate with a piece of bread and smiled at Iris. 'Lovely meal thanks, dear. That was Mac Wilson's beast. Very tasty.'

Iris glanced from one man to the other, her face worried.

Saul stood up and scraped his plate into the bin.

'Oh, you can't have had enough yet, Saul.' Iris pointed to the platter of sliced meat.

'No. I'm fine, thank you.'

His father got up and left his plate on the table.

Saul rinsed his plate and thought of how his father had never taken to Mae. He was friendly to her but it seemed to Saul that he was always watching her out of the corner of his eye, as if he could tell that she would never settle for life as a farmer's wife and she was simply biding her time in the valley. Saul suddenly remembered overhearing his father up at the meat co-op one evening soon after Mae's pregnancy became common knowledge around the valley. The men used to meet at the small timber cottage to do maintenance on the place. Once, Saul was out the back, smoking a stolen cigarette, and he could hear Mae's father inside, talking, as he had for days, of driving out west to track down the balloon man, at whichever small-town Show was on. Saul had put an eye to a crack in the door just as his dad interrupted

Mae's father, 'Forget it Jim. It'd do no good. You couldn't prove anything and the scoundrel wouldn't do the right thing by the little tart anyway.' Only one of Mae's uncles had looked shocked, glancing around the room as if waiting for a reaction. None of the other men seemed to notice what his father had called her. They kept talking, complaining about the rubbish left behind after the Show every year. Saul had thrown his cigarette onto the cement path and walked home along the road feeling sick, the gravel releasing the day's heat and the crickets pumping their noise into the evening air. He had climbed into bed fully clothed, his father's words replaying in his head, the most alone he had felt since his mother died.

He put his plate in Iris's fancy wooden dish rack and walked out onto the verandah. She called after him, 'Don't you want a cuppa Saul?'

'No thanks, Iris, I'll head off now.' He started down the steps. 'Thanks for dinner.'

He walked along his forest path and had the crazy idea that Allie would be waiting for him again. He had felt a mixture of delight and dread seeing her on his doorstep that morning and had wanted to ask her exactly how Mae died, wanted to demand specifics, quiz her about the whispers around the valley. All he had was an image of Mae gliding through the water, her arms tiring, moving slower and slower until she simply stopped swimming and let herself drift lazily to the bottom of the harbour. Julia was the one to ask but she had avoided him at the funeral. Of course he would never ask Allie. That morning at his place, she'd had the same slightly stunned expression as the day before at the graveside.

He had been standing across from her and his shadow had fallen down into Mae's grave but stopped short of the girl where she stood on the other side. It surprised him how deep the grave was. He had never imagined his mother buried that far down.

He remembered his father kneeling by his bed the morning of his mother's funeral, asking him if he wanted to go and somehow he knew that his dad didn't want him there. So he stayed with Mrs Jenkins down the road and waited the day through, in the slow heat and buzzing of cicadas. In the afternoon he had walked down towards the creek and heard the other kids yelling and hooting as they got off the school bus, then the splashes as they jumped into the waterhole. He had never forgotten the blank look on his father's face when he came to pick Saul up. It was as if he wasn't sure which house he was in, or what he was there for. Saul had been afraid that his father had already forgotten her, his face seemed so vacant.

His mother used to let him stand on a chair beside her while she cooked, a tea towel wrapped around his waist like an apron, the skirt reaching down his bare legs. One day—it was perfectly clear in his memory— he was carefully measuring three cups of flour into the big mixing bowl and when he finished he looked up and found her watching him, tears running down her cheeks. He stood motionless on his chair, small hands dusty with flour, waiting for her to reassure him but she had just rubbed the butter and flour together, crying still, her tears falling into the scone dough. He never saw her cry again. Even when they took her to hospital for the last time she had just held his hand to her cheek and smiled. He wished he could recall eating those last scones they had made.

Now Mae and his mother were in the town cemetery, the last traces of them turning to the one mass of soil. Mae had come over with her own mother once when his mother was very sick. They appeared on the doorstep with a casserole and a banana cake wrapped in a checked tea towel. It was the first time that Saul had really noticed Mae. They must have been seven and eight years old and were sent outside to play. They had run down to the creek, away from the quiet, serious house. He remembered sprinting, following her flashing legs across the bright grass and he wanted her to keep running, to lead him away from his grey-faced mother and silent father. They squatted on the bank of the creek and watched the eel swimming lazily around the waterhole until Mae stripped to her underpants and climbed the big tree to swing out on the thick rope his dad had tied to a branch. When the creek was muddy green from their jumping, they stretched out on the grass to let their undies dry. As he lay there, in the drowsy heat, flies tickling his skin, he watched her from the corner of his eye, the neat mound under her white cotton underpants and the way the tiny blonde hairs on her arm stirred in the breeze.

'I helped make the casserole,' she said as she lay back with her eyes closed. 'I chopped the carrots, so you can think of me when you eat the carrots.'

He didn't go to see her until the baby was almost due. From the orchard, he had watched the bleached white bed sheet blowing back against her body, outlining the great curve of her belly. All he could see were her hands slowly pegging the sheet on the line and her calves and feet in leather sandals. Then she pushed the cane basket with her foot and moved along the clothesline and into sight. He had forgotten how well he knew that face and the way her long hair slipped from where she tucked it behind her ear. He wanted to remember every detail of her moving in the sunlight, the white sheets flapping around her.

Then she saw him and dropped a wet sheet to the ground.

He called across to her, 'Mae. I just want to talk. I want to understand why you went off with him. I thought...'

She turned away and hurried inside, leaving the sheet crumpled on the grass.

He was backing out from under the lemon tree when Julia came out the door, thin and awkward in her school uniform. Her voice was apologetic. 'She says don't come again. Don't dare come again.'

'I just want to see her. I want to talk to her.'

'She's crying. I think you frightened her... ' She pulled at the loose hem of her dress. 'She's pretty jumpy these days.'

He walked away, looking back, hoping for a glimpse of her face at the window. There was nothing but Julia stretching up to hang out the last of the washing.

After the baby came, he tried again. Julia was waiting on the verandah as he swung open the wire gate. 'Bloody hell, Saul. Go away, will you? Dad's around.'

He nodded and kept walking up the path. 'Is she here?' He tried to see past her, through the open door.

'Wait. I'll go and find out if she'll see you.'

He could hear a distant clanging from the dairy and the cows lowing. It was nearly milking time and he couldn't stay long. Nerves pressed on his bladder and he looked around for somewhere to piss.

Then she was there and the sight of her stilled everything. All his prepared words were gone. He could see her dark nipples through the dress and even as he looked up at her where she stood on the verandah, they leaked milk onto the flimsy fabric. She was the same, still the same smooth tanned arms and slender fingers. Julia was standing in the doorway holding the baby and whispering to it, like Mae used to do to him down by the creek, his head in her lap, her hand stroking the hair back from his forehead.

She spoke first, 'How are you Saul?'

He opened his eyes wide to stop the tears. 'Mae.' Just to say her name was enough, just to stand watching her, then he remembered what he had come to say, 'I'm sorry. I'm sorry about what happened down the creek. I didn't mean...'

She looked down and shook her head. 'It doesn't matter. It was nothing...' She turned to Julia and motioned her to go inside.

His voice was soft. 'What happened? I don't understand what happened.'

Still looking down, she nodded. 'I miss you Saul.'

He took a breath. 'I just wish things were like they were before. If only this hadn't happened... it's just the thought of you with him... makes me...' His voice rose, 'I can't understand it. I don't understand why. It just feels so unfair.'

She squatted down on the verandah so her head was

level with his. He could smell her sweat and a new sweetness. He longed to press his face against the slope of her soft breasts.

She looked straight at him and whispered with an unfamiliar ferocity, 'It feels unfair to me too, Saul... It *is* unfair.' Her dark eyes locked on his. The baby started crying inside and she put a hand to her breasts and looked away. 'It's just the way it is,' she said. 'It'll all be okay. It'll be okay in the end.'

Saul stepped back. 'When's the end? I just want it the way it was, it was okay then...'

She interrupted him, holding a hand up. 'I have to go to the baby,' she pointed over her shoulder. 'I have to take care of her. I have no choice.'

He stepped forward and reached his hand out to touch her neck. She looked at him and whispered, 'No. Please don't... Saul. Please.' Then she let him brush his fingers against the loose strands of hair falling from her clip. Her skin was warm and damp under his fingers. He wanted to tangle his fingers in her hair and pull her back to him. She leaned into his hand for a moment before he loosened his grip, then she stood up and moved away from him into the house and didn't turn to look at him from the door like she used to.

chapter eleven

Julia walked down to the creek, naming the saplings out loud as she passed them. Quandong. Silky Oak. Native Tamarind. All her babies, growing taller and stronger now, populating the paddocks like the cows once did. She used to love the cows, so quiet and steadfast. She'd had a moment of regret as she watched the last one clatter up the ramp onto the cattle truck but it was time for the farm to sink back into the mud.

On the grassy bank, she stood watching the water tumble down the hill to join the main creek. She felt safest with her trees, digging holes and scooping the red earth with her hands. White Cedar. Red Ash. Foambark. She was calling them in, calling them back home. Their seeds would be carried along in the floods, like the big one she could sense coming. The tiny seeds tumbling through rapids and over causeways, waiting for the waters to subside so they could embed in a new land.

She squatted and hugged her knees. She wanted to

hold a warm body, like she used to hold the poddy calves, wriggling bags of bones with liquid black eyes. She and Mae would sneak down to the shed to cuddle them, sure of their father's scorn, but the one time he found them there he had simply smiled and gone to the bench for a tool.

Neal would hold her so tightly she could hardly breathe, and even if she'd wanted to escape his embrace, she couldn't. She was never afraid of him, even the first time, when she woke in the forest and found him standing over her, looking down with those pale blue eyes. When he left to go up north, he had promised to bring her back jars of mysterious dark seeds. She liked to picture him walking silently through the forest, turning his big bearded head to look up at the massive trees.

She hadn't been up to their cave since he left, afraid that the sand on the cave floor would still hold their footprints and the shape of their bodies where they had lain, the heat and weight of his body making her feel small. For years she had heard talk of him, the guy who lived in the forest and set traps for feral cats and foxes. She had even come across his hut one day, not long after her mother died. She was walking in the forest and smelt wood smoke, which led her to the hut tucked in at the foot of the bluff, with its neat tin roof and walls and chopped wood stacked under a small lean-to. Smoke drifted from the outside fireplace and she stood watching it for a few minutes, wondering if he would appear, then continued on her way through the bush.

The day she woke from her nap in the forest to find him watching her, he started speaking as if they were resuming a previous conversation. 'Did you know that you don't move when you sleep? Not at all. That's very unusual.'

She sat up. 'Is it?'

'I don't move either, apparently.' He looked up at the tree above her. He had a wide bushy beard and sat with his hands resting in his lap, a great stillness about him. 'You chose a good tree to sleep under. I've been collecting seed from her for years. She seeds in the summer.'

Julia looked up at the sinewy grey trunk and branches. She often escaped the farm to come and lie under this tree. This perfect tree. 'Could I have some of her seed?'

He nodded and got up. 'I'll bring you some. Another day.'

'How will you find me?'

He smiled. 'I'll find you,' and he had walked off, disappearing into the shadows of the forest.

She glanced up at the house to see if Allie was back yet. Julia was waiting again, like she used to wait for Mae. The day after the funeral, she had walked over to Saul's to warn him about Allie's night-time visit but he wasn't home. There were two empty teacups on the verandah—his mother's old rose bone china—and hanging on the back of a chair was one of Mae's thin crocheted cardigans that Allie had started wearing. Julia had picked up the cardigan, thinking she would take it home and drop it on Allie's bed, but as she started down the stairs she had turned and tossed it back towards the chair.

Now Allie wanted Saul to come to the birthday party. He and Julia had seen very little of each other since he returned to the valley and she dreaded him coming to the party and walking around the house trailing memories of Mae.

Whenever Julia saw him, in town or when she collected milk from his Dad, she felt a flush of embarrassment for how much she had wanted him when she was younger, and how obvious it had been. How she had longed for his shining face, the perfect curve of his muscles, his innocence. Even Julia could see how innocent he was. It wasn't fair that Mae chose him—there were other boys who wanted Mae. Older boys like the dark-haired second cousin from town who came, slim-hipped and knowing, to deliver gas bottles.

When Saul came back from Tasmania, Julia realised that nothing about him stirred her anymore. He wasn't innocent these days, just unimaginative, still willing to get up at four a.m. to work for his father although Julia knew that they barely broke even. He was too willing to slip back into the valley ways.

A couple of weeks after he returned, Julia was collecting milk and cream from his father while Saul cleaned out the dairy after a long morning's milking. She called across to him as he scrubbed out a vat, 'What on earth possessed you to get back into this dreadful routine, Saul?'

He walked towards her, smiling. 'There's something about it I enjoy, you know, I missed it when I was away… the cows, the dawn…'

She shook her head and started out the door with her plastic jug of milk.

His voice sharpened. 'You kept the dairy going after your father's accident. What's the difference?'

She replied as she walked away, 'The difference is that I loathed it.'

'So why did you do it?' he called after her.

She crossed the yard, knowing he was leaning in the door watching her. She had once dreamt of telling Saul, telling everything to his calm smiling face and she had woken from the dream with her heart pounding and, for a moment, filled with an incredible relief.

He waved at her as she drove out, an amused smile on his face. It didn't matter to her if they all thought she was crazy, it kept them at a quite satisfactory distance.

She squatted and cleared the grass from around one of her trees. It had a flush of tender green leaves and she imagined its roots working their way deep into the soil. There were thousands of her trees now, spreading like a balm on the land. She wiped her hands on her pants, picked up her bag of lemons and started back to the house. Her mother would have known how to organise a birthday party for Allie. She tried to remember her own fifteenth birthday but couldn't recall a thing. Mae would have been gone two years by then, and her mother was just starting to get ill, short of breath and tired all the time. On Julia's eleventh birthday, Mae had tied a rope to the head of her bed, and when Julia woke, as Mae was getting ready for milking, she found it, a line of rough twisted hemp leading out of the bedroom, through the house and down the steps, across the yard, to a bulky parcel of newspaper. Inside layers of paper was the china doll of Mae's that Julia had coveted for years. Mae's rope had led her straight into the dark little dairy storeroom that Julia had long since boarded up. 'Did you go in?' Mae had asked when Julia came back to the house cradling the doll. 'Did you go right into the storeroom?' Julia had clutched the doll and refused to answer.

Inside the house, Julia put on an apron and started squeezing the lemons, imagining Mae making lemon sponge pudding for Allie in that poky little kitchen in Sydney. She had been surprised how little evidence there was of Mae in the house, surprised that they had been living there for six years. It seemed like they had just moved in, with no pictures on the walls and cardboard boxes still stacked in corners.

She separated the eggs, sliding the bright yolk from shell to shell. She was making the pudding from memory. Before she died, her mother had destroyed her handwritten recipes and written them in code on index cards. Julia still couldn't interpret some of the symbols, strange curling shapes obscured by an old butter or jam smear. Julia's grandmother had given her some of the recipes but Julia suspected that she had changed a few key measurements, because they never turned out quite right. If Mae had asked, she would have been given the correct recipe. No-one ever denied that Mae was the favourite.

When their father came back from the hospital after the accident, still drugged, he couldn't believe that Mae had run away while he had been gone, and he kept asking for her. 'What do you mean she's not here? That's crazy.' It was when he came off the medication that he got angry and forbade them to speak of her. Years later, just before he finally died, Julia would wake in the night to his ramblings and sometimes stood at his bedroom door, listening. 'Mae, Mae, sweetheart,' he said in a voice that gripped her heart. He fought death all the way, railing at it in his sleep, rearing up in bed, his thin arms flailing.

She went to the chook house for another egg and saw Allie coming up the paddock, the wind pressing her dress against her body. She was smaller than Mae, but had her same loose-limbed walk, as if she was gliding across the ground. Julia called to her, 'Come and grab these for me, will you?'

Allie held out her skirt for the eggs that Julia passed through the wire door.

'I'm baking a trial lemon sponge pudding, to be sure I get it right for your birthday. Can't think of the last time I made it.'

Allie nodded. 'We used to have it lots. Usually on Sundays.'

Julia reached into a straw-filled nesting box. 'Have you been at Saul's?'

'Yeah.' Allie lifted a still-warm egg to her cheek.

'So he knows you were there?'

'Yes, of course he does.' She widened her eyes at Julia.

'What do you talk about?'

'Why do you want to know?'

'Just curious,' Julia felt her face reddening. She flicked dried chicken shit from an egg. 'You're not hassling him, are you?'

Allie glared at her. 'No!'

'Just lay off a bit, huh? Don't go there every day. He's got his own life, you know.'

Allie spun around and let the eggs fall from her skirt as she stalked across the yard to the house.

Julia looked at the glistening mess of yolks on the ground and leaned back against the door to the chook pen. She fixed her eyes on the birds pecking for grain in their muddy yard, their beaks and combs bright and glossy. Then she bent the wire catch shut and pushed her finger into the sharp end until a pearl of blood came.

For months Mae had lain in the bed beside Julia's, keeping it to herself. The morning that it all came out, Mae wouldn't get out of bed to do the milking. She lay still and silent when her father lifted the top sheet off her.

'Come on, Mae. No games this morning, please.' He folded the sheet into a neat square while he waited.

Julia watched through almost-shut eyes, the overhead light blinding.

Mae rolled over. 'I'm sick, Dad.'

He reached down and pulled her up by her arm. Instead of gathering herself and getting up like she usually did, Mae let her body swing out from her father's grip. The sleeve of her yellow nightie caught on the bedpost and ripped. She started to cry, which shocked Julia more than the way her father suddenly dropped Mae to the floor.

'Fine.' He pointed at Julia, 'You can help with the milking, then. It's about time you pulled your weight. Helping your mother is not enough.'

From where she lay in bed, Julia looked up at him and at her mother who had appeared in the doorway, a questioning look on her face. Her mother stopped tying her apron. 'Mae? What's wrong sweetheart?'

'Nothing. Nothing. I'm getting up,' Mae's voice was shaky with tears and she got onto her knees. Julia wanted her to stand up and not stay there on all fours like a dog.

Julia went out onto the verandah and stepped into her gumboots. Mae appeared and followed her father down the steps. He unchained the dog and the two of them walked across the dark yard as they did every morning.

Julia went after them, the damp air cooler than she had expected. Her mother appeared beside her. 'Are you going to help with the milking too, Mum? Why does he need all of us?' Julia longed to be back in bed.

Her mother called out, her voice unusually commanding. 'Mae!'

Mae turned back.

Their father looked at his wife, his eyebrows raised. 'Well, I'll get the cows in! Julia, seeing you're here, you put the barley out.' He opened the gate and walked into the dark paddock, his torch sweeping before him.

Their mother walked over to Mae and took her arm. 'I think I know why you're sick.'

Mae started to cry again, her head dropping down.

'How long since your last menses?'

Mae's voice was quiet. 'Four months, maybe five.'

'Five months! Mae! Why haven't you said anything? Does Saul know?'

She shook her head. 'It's not him.'

'Go down and do what your father asked, Julia.' Her mother pointed to the dairy, where the cows were waiting. Julia could hear her father calling to the barking cattle dog. She couldn't move. Nothing seemed real, this conversation her mother and Mae were having, Mae crying. All four of them down at the dairy in the dark.

Mae took a breath. 'It was a man from the Show.'

'Did he take you by force?' Her mother's face was shocked.

Mae shrugged then shook her head and lifted her

hands to cover her eyes. Her mother took Mae into her arms. 'What a mess.'

Their father came into the yard. 'Julia! Have you put the barley out?' He stopped at the sight of Mae in her mother's arms. 'What's going on?'

No-one spoke. Julia slipped past him and in the dairy door.

'I said, what... is... going on?' When there was no reply, his voice turned hard. 'Mae, go and start the milking.'

Mae pulled her mother's arms off her and walked silently back towards the house.

He roared, his voice shocking in the still morning. 'I said get inside there and start work, Mae! Do you hear me?'

'I'll do it,' Julia's mother took a step towards the dairy. 'I'll do it.'

He shook his head and grabbed her arm. 'Stop, Bess. I want an explanation. Now.'

Julia watched from the dairy door as her parents looked at each other. Behind them Mae was already walking up the steps into the house.

'She's pregnant.' Her mother looked away.

There was a long silence. Julia waited, fear for all of them tightening in her stomach. The cows shuffled behind her and the dog slumped at her feet and scratched itself. She wanted to run after Mae.

Her father was still staring at her mother. He turned and walked into the dairy. 'Get out of here Julia. You're bloody useless. Get back to the house.'

Julia ran across the yard. At the top of the steps she turned and looked back—there were the familiar sounds from the dairy and in the sky, apricot streaks and a light blue glow. It was one of the most beautiful and most awful sunrises she had ever seen.

chapter twelve

The old woman stood waiting at the front door, looking around her at the plastic pots piled high on the verandah and the weeds growing up through the boards. Her disdain was clear to Allie even from where she sat perched in the branches of the mulberry tree.

'Grandma!' Julia called from the paddock.

'Oh,' the old woman walked to the end of the verandah. 'There you are. I've tried to phone you a thousand times, Julia, but you don't answer.'

Julia came up the path shaking her head. 'No, no. I've been planting down the paddock. Come inside. Time for a break anyway.' She pulled off her boots and pushed the door open.

Allie slid down out of the tree and stood at the open window looking in. The old woman was wearing a pink dress and her shoes seemed too big for her thin legs. This was Mae's beloved grandmother, putting down her worn handbag and picking up the wooden casing of an old clock Julia had taken apart. 'I've been waiting for you to ring me about coming down for lunch so I could see my great-granddaughter but I have to take things into my own hands, obviously.' She smiled and put the clock down. 'Where is she?'

Julia put the kettle on the stove and said, 'I don't know. I think she's grumpy at me.'

'Why doesn't that surprise me, Julia?'

Julia dropped the burnt match into the bin. 'Do you want Earl Grey or Orange Pekoe?'

The old woman walked up close to Julia and adjusted the kettle on the stove. 'It's as if you don't want to be part of the family anymore, Julia. Something about you has changed. And I wouldn't bring it up except for Allie. She needs to feel her whole family around her.'

'She hasn't asked to see you, Grandma. And no, nothing about me has changed.' Julia turned to face her. 'Actually, who I am now is who I've always really been.'

'Don't talk nonsense Julia, I've known you since you were born. I've known you since before you knew yourself.' She sighed. 'Look, I can see you sacrificed for your mother and father, for the farm, but that didn't mean you had to relinquish all ideas of marriage or family. Now it's like you are just going on being deliberately contrary and difficult.'

'This is what I want.'

'This?' she waved her hand around. 'This is something to aspire to? The farm is falling apart. This house needs a family. Joe Hogan wanted you.'

'Joe Hogan wants his meals cooked and laundry done… like Dad wanted from Mum and then from me. Didn't we already have this discussion several times when

Joe was scouting for a wife?'

'It's not just about you anymore. If you want to reject your family that's one thing. But now Allie's involved too. She's part of Mae that's come back to the valley.'

Julia sighed and reached for the tea canister.

'Where is she Julia? I'll go and find her.'

Allie stepped inside the door as the old woman turned and saw her, 'Oh. There you are. Yes.' She pulled something out of her bag and passed it to Allie. For a second Allie thought it was a photo of herself, then she saw that it was Mae, with long dark plaits, standing unsmiling and straight-backed in front of a white paling fence, a skinny fair kid beside her.

The old woman came close, the sweetness of her perfume overpowering. 'That's Julia with her, believe it or not.' She tapped on the photo with a short fingernail. 'Mae's twelve here. Just started high school. You know she was the brightest girl in the school. She really could have done anything. The teachers all said that.'

There was a seriousness in her mother's face that Allie had never seen, and her eyes were wide open, as if searching for all the possible futures that lay ahead.

The old woman reached for Allie's hand and stroked it with her papery fingers. 'Did she ever talk about coming back to the valley? This farm is half hers you know. Half yours now, I should think.' She raised her voice. 'Isn't that right Julia? Allie has a right to half this property.'

Julia shrugged and prised open a tin of shortbreads. 'I don't know. I haven't looked into the legalities of it.'

'You'd better. Allie may not like what you are doing

to the place. It doesn't even look like a farm anymore.'

'That's the idea.'

'So you say.' The old woman started getting down china teacups and saucers from the kitchen dresser. 'Let's drink from these, Julia. I can't abide those thick cups you use.'

Julia nodded as she slipped a knitted cosy over the teapot.

Allie moved close to the old woman and spoke quietly, so Julia wouldn't hear. 'She always read the *National Geographics* you sent.'

She tilted her head and smiled, 'I thought so.'

Julia put a jug of milk on the table. 'What *National Geographics*?'

'I used to send Mae magazines when we'd finished with them.'

'You did? I didn't know you had contact with her.'

The old woman shrugged her shoulders and sat down at the table. She patted at her short white hair.

Julia said, 'So how often did you send magazines to her?'

'Often enough. But you'll no doubt be pleased to hear, Julia, that she only ever wrote back to me once.' She tipped the milk jug to look inside. 'Who are you getting your milk from these days?'

'The Philips.'

Allie wanted to tell her great-grandmother that Mae used to stack the magazines in the toilet outside, the pile of yellow spines growing higher and higher over the years. Mae would tear out articles and leave them on Allie's pillow. In the dust under her bed was a tangle of screwed-up stories about Antarctic adventurers and

African tribes. Mae's grandmother also sent tea towels, fine Irish linen that Mae would carefully iron and stack in the kitchen cupboard. She pressed all their sheets and pillowslips. She even took on an ironing job for a little while but they said she was too slow. Allie looked down at the photo of her mother, to see again that clear light in her face.

The old woman poured the tea. 'I saw you talking to young Saul Philips the other day. I guess you heard about him and your mother, how they were sweethearts?'

Allie nodded. 'She told me.'

'So who is this Tom that Julia mentioned? I notice he didn't turn up for the funeral.'

Allie glanced at Julia as she spoke. 'Maybe he didn't hear about it.'

The old woman raised her eyebrows. 'Just like Mae never heard about her own mother's funeral?'

Julia's voice was low. 'How was I supposed to get in contact with her if I didn't have a phone number or street address? It's Mae's fault for being so bloody secretive and for not checking her post box for days! The only reason she made it to Dad's funeral was because I insisted she give me her actual address after she never turned up to Mum's. I had to wring it out of her like…' She flapped her hands into the air as she stood up and went to the bench.

'Just the same, she should have been here for her mother's burial. We needed her here.' The old woman gripped Allie's hand again, 'So was Tom going to marry her? She could have had any man she wanted you know. She was like her father in that, he had all the women in the valley after him. What was he like, this Tom?'

Tom who had bent to wipe the drops of blood from the floor, the very last traces of her mother. She hated that she had let him hold her that morning when Mae disappeared. Right there at the bottom of the stairs he had hugged her to his pale flesh. She looked down at the photo on her lap.

Julia said, 'Grandma... I don't think this is quite the time...'

'I hardly need your instruction on social etiquette, my dear.'

Julia stood up and poured more hot water into the teapot.

'I'd like you to come and visit me in town, Allie. We have a spare room, your great-uncle Dan and I. You can stay with us as long as you want. Anytime, for as long as you want. There was always an open invitation to your mother too, you know.'

Allie remembered when she and Mae came up for Allie's grandfather's funeral. Early the first morning, Mae had walked out into the paddock, her shadow stretching behind her, her black shoes wet from the grass, and she had suddenly dropped to the ground and pressed her hands into the earth. 'I never thought I missed it. Not like this.' And she had gripped her stomach and doubled over as she waved Allie away. 'Leave me alone. Go back to the house.'

The old woman put down her teacup. 'Don't fill the pot for me Julia. I've got to keep going, I happened to be out here delivering a meal to the Lachlans and I'm due back in town. I just wanted to drop that photo off to Allie.' She stroked Allie's hair. 'Keep it. And come and visit me soon, eh?'

Allie followed her aunt out to the old woman's car. Julia waved as the car disappeared down the driveway, then she turned and walked briskly down the paddock, pulling her gloves back on.

Allie went inside and picked up the half-eaten shortbread left on her great-grandmother's plate. She put a piece on her tongue and let it dissolve into a sweet paste. She remembered that at her grandfather's funeral, Mae had sought out the old woman and hugged her a long time, her eyes squeezed tight.

Mae hadn't wanted Allie to go with her to the funeral. She had arranged for Allie to stay with a neighbour but when she took her down there with her bag, the neighbour came to the door and said her husband was sick and there was no way she could look after Allie as well, so the two of them ended up catching the afternoon train north. Allie knew from the way Mae stared out the train window that she didn't want to talk.

Mae had embarrassed her by crying when she hugged Julia on the station platform. Allie could see people glancing sideways as they walked around the two women to collect their luggage. She had been surprised that Julia was so much bigger than Mae. She was taller and broader in her blue work pants, her face clean of make-up, her fine pale hair long and loose down her back. In the front seat of Julia's old ute, Allie sat between her aunt and her mother, Julia's thigh pressed against her leg, tensing then softening as her aunt changed gears.

Mae smoked a cigarette, half-leaning out the window, her voice whisked away with the smoke as they drove across the river flats towards the hills. 'So how did it happen?' She spoke to Julia the same way she spoke to

Allie, straight down the line with none of the lightness in her voice that she used with Tom.

'Just like that. It just happened,' said Julia. 'I went in after milking and all the blankets were off, he'd thrown them on the floor, and his arms were out, like this.' She stretched one arm along in front of Allie and Mae. 'He was so thin in the end, you could see where the bones had been broken in the accident, they'd all... calcified,' her voice dropped. Allie was afraid she would cry again. 'He was so thin, Mae... and just completely cold when I went in. He must have been like that all night. I should have checked on him before milking.'

There was silence as the car climbed the escarpment, the engine churning slowly around the steep hairpin bends, up and away from the plain and wide river. As they drove along the ridge in the fading light, Allie peered out at the dark forest reaching over the road. She spoke into the silence. 'What accident?'

'What?' said Mae.

'What accident broke his bones?'

Julia flicked on the wipers, as light rain sprinkled the windscreen. Allie waited for her mother to speak but it was Julia who said, 'Dad had a tractor roll on him.'

'How? How did it roll on him?'

'He drove it wrong, made a mistake.'

'Did he go to the same hospital I was born in?'

'Yes,' Mae sighed, exhaling smoke. 'The very same. You were born there and he ended up there a few weeks later.' She threw her cigarette butt onto the road and wound up the window against the rain. She rubbed Allie's thigh and her hand pressed too hard.

Allie shut her eyes and turned her head from side to side to smell one and then the other sister—the cigarette smoke, the perfume and the mustiness. As they descended into the valley, the forest opened out into wide paddocks, vivid green in the last light of the day. Allie leaned into her mother and whispered, 'Where's he live? The First Love?'

But Mae pursed her lips and shook her head.

chapter thirteen

It was difficult for Allie to see him in the dark but there was the faint smell of incense and the soft intake of his breath. It was the most intimate sound of him, the breath moving in and out of his body. Creatures rustled in the big mango tree beside his house. She liked being in the forest at night, the sounds of other life going on all around her, the clickings and scurryings of small animals.

Her eyes found the outline of his body where he lay on his back, his hair dark on the white pillow. People's faces were naked while they slept. Mae seemed sad when she was asleep, the corners of her mouth pulled down, a faint crease between her thin eyebrows. Allie wanted to shine her torch onto Saul's face. What she was looking for might be written on his face.

She put her hands on the wooden windowsill and pulled herself up so she could lean her body into the air of his room. The sill creaked under her and he stirred.

She dropped to the ground and heard the sheets rustling and then his footsteps through the house.

His front door banged shut and he was coming down the steps, pulling a T-shirt over his head. 'Allie?'

The pulse in her neck ticked as he walked across the wet grass towards her. How inevitable it felt, this circling to the truth, like the stars wheeling their way across the sky. She and Mae used to lie back and watch the night sky turning around them.

He stood in front of her, his voice sharp. 'What are you doing here?'

She looked up at him. 'I can't sleep.'

He turned to look out at the forest, his hands on his hips. 'So what are you doing here, at my house?'

Her mouth was dry. 'I don't know.'

He squatted beside her. There was the fuggy smell of sleep on him. 'You frightened me. I don't want you looking in on me in the middle of the night. Come and visit me during the day but not like this.'

'I was just walking. If I walk then I can go back and sleep.'

He was silent for a moment. 'You know that Mae used to walk at night? She'd come to my window and chuck stones at it and I'd go out and we'd sit on the verandah under my mum's old mosquito net.'

'She never told me that.'

'I thought that was why you'd come.' He smiled. 'So, maybe she didn't tell you everything after all.'

'She told me everything important.'

He looked at her for a moment, then said, 'Did she tell you that I went to Sydney?'

'What?'

'I went looking for her, I tracked her down.'

'No! I don't believe you. She would have said.' She swayed a little on her haunches and reached back to the warm brick pier behind her.

'It's true. She'd been gone two years and I was on my way back down to Tasmania and I just got off the train in Sydney and went looking for her.'

'You found her?' Allie sat down and the damp ground soaked through her thin cotton dress.

'Yeah. I found you both. You were little, a toddler. I waited at the post office and eventually she came to pick up her mail. She was unwrapping a package on the steps and I sat down next to her.'

'And?'

'And we went and had a milkshake at a place just down from the post office.'

'The Parthenon.' She shook her head. 'I was there?'

'Yeah.'

'But I don't remember! I'd remember.' He had come to find her, actually come to claim her and Mae never said anything.

'You were only little.' He threaded his fingers together. 'Maybe she never told you because it was kind of awkward. We ended up arguing, there in the bloody milk bar… while the guy cooked hamburgers and chips five feet away.'

'What did you argue about?'

He lifted his hands into the air. 'It just wasn't… I just wanted to make contact with her, you know.' He was measuring his words. 'I thought I could put something to rest, I guess. But she was kind of nervous. I think that the guy, what's his name… Tom, must have been on the scene and I guess she was worried about getting home to him. She kept saying she had to get home, that she was expected. Then she just stood up, and said that I was crazy and that she couldn't just pick up and try again somewhere else, it was just too hard and I should go off and find myself a good wife.'

'What was too hard? What did she mean, it was too hard?'

He shrugged. 'Things hadn't exactly been easy.'

'But Tom wasn't around then. She didn't meet him till I was like five or six!'

'I don't know, then. I didn't understand it.' He stretched one leg out in front of him and leaned back against the house.

Allie was silent, looking up at the clouds scudding across the sky, letting moonlight leak through. 'Don't you think she would have been a good wife?'

He nodded slowly, 'Yeah.' He emphasised each word, 'She would have. She was a good woman.'

'Is that what you wanted? Did you want her to be your wife?'

He took a moment to reply. 'Not then. Not when I went to Sydney, that wasn't what I was trying to... I just wanted to see her, that's all.'

Allie shielded her face as a flying fox swooped low in front of them, its black wings buffeting the air. It landed in the dark shape of the tree above them. How could Mae have not told her? Day after day, Mae had let her wait for him.

A mango dropped to the ground in front of them. Saul reached over to pick it up. 'Not ripe yet. Iris always wants me to pick them for her but I prefer to leave them for the bats and the local kids. This tree has been here at least eighty years, the original homestead on the property was down here. All the kids come every summer. These are the best mangoes in the valley.' He tossed the fruit into the bushes. 'Once, when I was little, maybe in second or third class, I came down here one day and there was a group of boys teasing this little kid. They started beating him up, pelting him with rotten mangoes and stones. He was a scrawny little guy, from a poor family up the valley. He'd come down with an old carry bag to get mangoes. And I did nothing, I just stood and watched. They wouldn't let him run away, so he just curled up in a ball while they pelted him. And a few times he looked over at me, while I just stood there. He works at the co-op in town now, he's a big guy with a beard and beer gut. I tried to apologise to him once. I started, you know, describing the incident and saying how sorry I was. And he just laughed and said I was confusing him with someone else.'

Allie stood up. He was worse than Mae, holding out on her, distracting her with stories. It was up to him to say it, she wasn't going to extract it from him as if it were some terrible confession. She spoke abruptly. 'Goodbye. Sorry I frightened you.'

He called after her, 'Hey!'

At the edge of the clearing she looked back. He was still sitting there, his face pale in the darkness, watching her.

When she was little she would use the back lane to get into the next-door neighbours' garden and look in their window. She was most interested in the father, the way he rolled his shirt sleeves up and let his hand rest on the head of his little girl as he talked to his wife. A golden light seemed to emanate from their house, the same warm light she saw in windows when she and Mae walked at night. Then one evening they saw her looking in at them and the father came out to where she stood in the dark garden. 'What are you doing?' he had asked. She couldn't recall what she said to him, but remembered his big hand warm and firm around hers as he led her home. Mae was lying upstairs listening to the radio. 'I don't want her lurking in our backyard,' he told Mae. She nodded and took Allie into the kitchen for a cup of hot chocolate. The next weekend, he put a lock on their back gate.

Lights blazed from the farmhouse and wood smoke hung in the damp air.

Julia was stoking the old wood stove and looked up when Allie walked in. 'Where have you been?'

'Out.' The kitchen was humming with heat and the smell of caramelising fruit.

'At midnight? Are you okay? You look pale.'

'I'm fine.' Mango skins and seeds were heaped on the table. She traced a finger through the sticky juice. 'Did you know Saul went to look for Mae and me in Sydney?'

Julia looked up from weighing dried fruit, her face shining with perspiration, 'Who told you that?'

'He did. She never said anything.' The heat in the room was tremendous and passed through her body as if she wasn't there. She sat down and stroked a glossy smooth mango. 'She kept…' Allie lifted her hands up as if holding a ball. 'She kept all this information…'

Julia nodded. 'Yeah. A lot of people do.' She tipped a dish of red glacé cherries into a big bowl and used her hands to mix them through the cake batter. 'Sorry it's so hot in here. I've always used the wood stove to bake the Christmas fruitcakes. I just normally do it earlier in the year when it's not so warm. Thought I'd make some mango chutney while we had the stove going.'

'She just let me wait for him to come! I used to listen to cars stopping on the street at night, thinking it was him. I'd sit on the front step watching strange men walking down the street, wondering if they were going to turn in at our gate. She just let me go on waiting.' Juice dripped through a crack in the table onto her leg. She remembered the milk bar run by the skinny Greek guy and his wife. Year after year Allie had walked across the lino and stood at the counter waiting for a parcel of chips and Mae never told her that the First Love had been there too. He should have tried harder and come back when she was old enough to recognise him. He owed it to her.

Julia shook her head and scraped the last of the thick cake mix into greased and papered tins. She slid them into the oven and went out onto the verandah, lifting her shirt and turning her body to meet the faint breeze. She called back to Allie, 'You know, sometimes the stories we tell are not for other people, they're for us. We're really telling them for ourselves.'

'She thought I couldn't tell which were the real stories. She thought I couldn't figure it out. I should have had him before now. I should have had him a long time ago.'

'What do you mean "had him"?'

'I mean I should have had a father.'

Julia tilted her head. 'You don't think he's your father?'

'I don't think it. I know it.'

'Oh no. No, he's not your father.' She shook her head vehemently, and stepped back inside. 'Bloody hell, he hasn't told you this, has he?'

'I just know it.'

Julia came close to her. 'Allie, he's not your father. Don't you think Mae would have wanted him to be? Don't you think it would have been easier for her if he was? Have you asked him? Ask him, he'll tell you.'

'You just don't want him to be. How would you know, anyway? I mean, what has any of this got to do with you?'

'God. I'm sorry. I should have realised this was what you were thinking,' Julia rubbed her face.

'It's nothing to do with you, Julia. I know what the truth is and he knows it too. You think you know Mae. You pretend you do but you know nothing about her. Nothing at all.'

She ran down the steps and into the paddock. She found one of the pathways through the weeds and hurried towards the light coming from Petal's caravan. As she walked into the dark dripping forest, she could see in the end window of the van. Between the red curtains there were two bodies, Petal and a man with the same long blonde hair, moving like one creature. She stood watching them, the same electricity in her body as when she used to hear Mae and Tom. She would try to block out the rhythmic, rocking sounds from upstairs, turning one ear into her pillow, but still the warmth would come, spreading between her legs like shameful hot urine, spreading while she listened for her mother's cry. The sound that came from her mother's lips would drop through the air and into her window.

She turned away from Petal's van and walked blindly into the black forest, branches and vines tearing at her skin.

The blood came in the middle of the night, black on her pants and thighs and fingertips. She sat on the toilet in the dark house, Julia's room quiet and the air still heavy with the sugary smell of cake. With one hand she gripped her wrist and looked down at her fingers, so thin and fragile, daubed in the blackness.

In the morning Julia gave her pads and she lay in bed, listening to the rain, the blood trickling stickily down the crack of her buttocks onto the sheet. Julia came in with a cup of milky tea and sat on the edge of the bed, her face soft. She patted Allie's leg through the sheet and the weight of her aunt's hand made hot tears rise behind her eyes. She rolled away from Julia and pulled the sheet up to her chin and traced her fingers down her side, following the lines of sweat, imagining them his fingers on Mae's skin. Julia was wrong about Saul. What would Julia know? She was only a girl when Mae and Saul were together.

She drifted back to sleep, the smells of Julia's cooking all around her. She dreamt of thick drops of blood sitting plump on the front path in Sydney. In the dream she was in Mae's nightdress, the cement digging into her knees as she bent to lick at the drops with her tongue. She licked until her tongue was raw, to take something of Mae into her, one last bit of her mother.

The pad was thick between her thighs. Neither Mae nor Julia had told her that the blood kept coming and coming or that the cotton wadding would be soaked in a few hours. When she undressed to have a bath, it skimmed a crimson line down her bare leg and dripped perfect shining circles onto the linoleum. Everything was blood—her skin, her underpants, the back of her dress, the sheets. It lay just under the skin of her whole body, like tears ready to burst.

Julia was watching her closely, leaning out the kitchen window to check on her where she sat on the verandah. Allie waited until she heard her aunt go into the bathroom, then she ran down the steps and into the forest.

His front door was unlocked, like last time. She stood on the threshold and looked around the room. He had left a towel hanging over the back of a chair and a stick of incense burned on the kitchen table, a thin thread of smoke rising into the air. Allie stepped inside and rubbed the silky ashes of the incense between her fingers.

In the bathroom, a razor balanced on the edge of the sink, trailing a line of tiny black whiskers and soap foam. She squeezed a bead of his toothpaste onto her finger and touched her tongue to its gritty sweetness before she walked across the hall to his bedroom, her bare feet whispering on the smooth floorboards. His bed was unmade, the sheets and pillows tangled. She riffled the pages of the book beside the bed and had a sudden pang for the long neat rows of books in the school library. A dog barked in the distance and a fly buzzed insistently against the window. She knelt and pressed her face into the mattress, silently mouthing their names to herself. Mae and Saul.

There were loud footsteps on the stairs and his voice, talking to the dog. She crossed to the open window and climbed out, dropping to a squat on the grass just as his dog ran down from the verandah towards her, wagging its tail. She walked up the stairs and met Saul coming out the front door. He had keys in one hand and was about to take a bite from an apple with the other.

'Hello again,' he said, raising his eyebrows.

'Where are you going?'

'Into town.' He started walking across the lawn then turned back to her. 'Do you wanna come?'

She nodded and followed him to his ute.

She wound down the car window to let the air onto her skin. The midday heat gathered around her and pricked behind her knees. Saul drove with one hand and took the corners fast. When the car reached the top of the escarpment, the clouds suddenly cleared and they could see right across the bare plain, past the town and looping river, to the sea glittering in the distance. She watched his hands loosely grip the wheel as he steered the ute down past the wind-shredded bananas onto the river flats. There was something so familiar about the square shape of his palm and the angle at the base of his thumb, as if she had always known it. She shut her eyes and tried to find the right words to prompt him.

He spoke suddenly into the silence, 'You know, I was thinking, maybe she didn't say anything about me going to Sydney because it was so complicated.' He smiled. 'Sometimes it's easier to keep things simple.'

'Yeah? I don't think complication was a concern for her.'

'What do you mean?'

She thought of Tom leaning back in his chair in the kitchen while Mae straddled him, her skirt cutting into her thighs, and how he had once reached up and deliberately smeared her red lipstick across her face.

'Like Tom. We'd never know when he was coming over. He'd come after work, or at midnight. And mostly he'd leave before dawn, so he'd be home and his kids wouldn't know he'd spent the night away.'

'His kids?'

'His wife knew about us. But he didn't want his kids to know...'

A herd of caramel-coloured cows was crossing the road. Saul slowed the car and put his arm out the window to wave to the farmer standing by the road. 'Hey Bill.'

The farmer nodded back as Saul edged the car forward past a cow that had separated from the herd and was lumbering down the road, her heavy udder swinging.

'His wife tracked him down once and found his car parked out the front. She stayed outside for hours and Mae and Tom hid inside, laughing. His wife didn't know which house was ours. She was just waiting for him to turn up...' She watched his face. 'Mae was never really in love with him.'

'How do you know?'

'She told me.' She didn't want to think about Tom. The sound of his voice from upstairs, loud, telling Mae to stop crying. Tom yelling down the stairs in the morning, 'Why didn't you take a fucking key, Mae?'

then coming down in his singlet and opening the door to the policeman.

Saul slowed the ute as they entered town and a solitary boy rode his bike across the pedestrian crossing, under a limp streamer of tinsel. Saul pulled up outside the old corner pub. Shapes moved in the gloom inside and there was the sound of laughter and glasses clinking. Upstairs on the wide verandah, a line of red-checked tea towels hung over the lace fretwork.

'What did you and Mae argue about when you came to find us? What did you talk about?'

He shook his head. 'I can't remember exactly. I guess we talked about us...'

'So why didn't you come again?' she said as a man in a faded brown felt hat left the pub and came towards Saul's open window.

'I... what was the point?'

'What do you mean, what was the point?'

The man reached them. 'Saul, mate. What you doing in from the hills? Big day in town, eh?'

Saul smiled at him and undid his seatbelt. 'Yeah, yeah. How ya goin' Mike? Mike this is Allie, Julia's niece.' He nodded at her and got out. 'I'll be back in a tick. I've just got to run in and get a bottle of brandy, then we can go over to the shop.'

She watched him disappear into the dark doorway and shut her eyes for a moment. A loud burst of laughter came from the pub. She hadn't been into town since the funeral, since Mae was buried under a ton of dirt, deep down where she could never be reached. The smell of bubbling tar rising from the road made her feel sick and she shifted so her back was towards the cemetery.

She lifted her thighs off the burning vinyl seat and rested them back onto her palms, the sweat slippery between her fingers.

She could just see the slow river drifting by on the far side of the park. Mae had told her how she used to visit friends in town and they would let the tide pull their little tin dinghy down the river towards the ocean, rowing and hanging a fishing line over the side until they reached the mouth of the river, where they tied up and bought hot chips from the fish co-op and swam all day in the lagoon before letting the turn of the tide take them back to town. Allie picked one of the houses fronting the river, with its wide verandahs and palm trees, and imagined her mother as a girl, running barefoot along the hot grass and in the front gate.

Saul came out of the pub carrying a brown paper bag and squinting his eyes against the sun. He stopped to talk to someone on the footpath and Allie suddenly didn't recognise anything about him, this short man with broad shoulders and muddy boots. For a moment, she didn't know how she could possibly be connected to this stranger, sitting in the front seat of a stranger's car, on a street in a strange town. Panic swelled in her chest and she shut her eyes to call up the vision of Mae trailing behind the dinghy on a lazy summer's day.

'Doing a big shop for Christmas are you then, Saul?' the man at the grocery shop weighed the dried fruit and tipped it into brown paper bags. He didn't wait for a reply. 'Can't see you in the kitchen cooking up a batch of mince tarts, but there you go. Nice to have a bit of sun then, isn't it? But doesn't it make things steamy?'

He wiped his hands on his apron and looked at Allie. 'Now you'd have to be a Curran, wouldn't you? You've definitely got the family look.'

Saul spoke, 'This is Allie. Julia's niece.'

The man bent to pick up a cardboard box. 'Julia's niece... ?' he said, then exclaimed, 'Oh!' just as Saul said, 'Mae's daughter.'

'Oh yes, of course. I remember.' He smiled at Allie again. 'Is it hot enough for you then?'

She nodded. She didn't like his oily grey hair slicked back, his too-white teeth. They each carried a box to the ute and the man tapped the bonnet as he turned to go back to the shop. 'Well, see you later then. Let's hope we get a bit more sun before the rain comes back.'

Saul pulled across the street and turned onto the road out of town. Massive old fig trees lined the road, dwarfing the neat timber houses. At the edge of town he pointed to a light blue house with a hedge of red hibiscus bushes. 'You know that's where your great-grandmother lives?'

'There?' The small house was quiet, the curtains drawn against the heat, an old white station wagon parked in the driveway. It was the last house before the wide unfenced cane fields.

She wanted him to stop so she could open her great-grandmother's front gate and walk up the neat cement path to the door, like Mae would have done if she were there. She would step into the cool dark living room and sit down on the couch beside the old lady.

He sped up as they left town. 'You asked me why I didn't go to see Mae again. She wouldn't have wanted to see me. It was... it wasn't great, that meeting we had.

It was clear…'

'So, why did you go the first time if you didn't want to get back with her?'

He frowned and shook his head, 'Oh. I'm not sure. It was just so awful the way it had all ended, up here in the valley. I wanted to understand…'

'So the point was to make you feel better.'

'Ahh, Allie,' he shook his head, his voice exasperated. 'I just wanted to see her, that's all.'

She spoke quickly, the words tumbling out, 'Did you ever think you might be my father?'

He slowed the car then pulled over onto the gravel beside the road. 'Is that what you've been thinking?' His face was serious, and he looked away from her for a moment. She could see each dark curl at the nape of his neck. 'I wanted to be,' he said as he turned back to her. 'I wanted to be your father. But I always knew I wasn't.'

'So you believed every single thing she said, did you?'

'It wasn't about what she said. I knew it.'

'But how…? How did you know it?' They were parked out the front of the town pool, a bright blue rectangle in the middle of the cane fields. In the silence that hung between them, there was the lonely sound of crows in the trees behind the pool. She kept her eyes on the chemical blue of the water, she didn't want to see him saying these words.

''Cause we never…' he shifted his legs. 'We didn't actually… have intercourse, you know. It wasn't…'

'You never had sex?'

He shook his head.

She wanted to get out into the shimmering heat and step over the small ditch of water beside the road and run down one of the narrow dirt tracks between the tall rows of cane, right to the centre of the vast field. She remembered very well Mae's descriptions of how gentle he was as they made love, his hands holding her so tenderly, the motion of their bodies together. Mae used to lie back in bed, her eyes shut, and tell Allie how they would wrap themselves in a blanket, the wool rough on their bare skin.

He put the car into gear and pulled back onto the road. 'I don't know what to say… I don't know what Mae told you. Maybe she wished it too, you know. I'm sorry.' He turned the car onto the road that led up into the hills. Heavy rain clouds were rolling down from the escarpment.

Allie's voice was blunt. 'Either she's lying or you are.'

'What did she tell you?'

'She told me lots. There'd be no reason for her to lie. Don't you think she'd know who got her pregnant?' Even as she spoke, she remembered how Mae used to change her stories over time, the description of the first kiss getting more and more detailed and changing location from the bank of the creek to a boulder. The truth was that Allie couldn't keep track of Mae's stories but she was sure that Mae had always meant her to know that the First Love was her father and the Balloon Man was just an invention.

He put his hand out the window, as if testing the air as it streamed past. 'Everyone knew it was him, Allie. People saw them at the Show together. She was upfront about it, she told everyone. Believe me.'

The wind was whipping up, spinning twigs onto the roof of the car and down onto the road. The air coming in the window was suddenly cooler. She could feel sticky blood on her inner thighs.

He said, 'I can help you find him if you like. I'll help you.'

'What? The Balloon Man?' He didn't even have a name. A nameless, faceless man that Mae never meant her to find. 'Why would you want to get involved? And if you're going to find him, what was his real name?'

His voice was soft, 'Didn't she tell you anything about him?'

'She told me about you.'

'I'll help you. If you want, I'll help you.' He sighed. 'Oh look, here comes the rain.' Fat drops split open on the windscreen like small ripe fruit and spattered through the window onto her hot bare legs.

chapter fourteen

When he pulled up, Allie leapt out without a word and ran towards the house, leaving the car door wide open to the rain. He sat, letting the rain wet the seat, watching her run down the path, long dark hair swinging, the shape of her exactly like Mae. Bloody Mae, what had she told her? He thought about getting out and going to speak to Julia, but he was already late for milking.

At his father's place, he parked under a tree and hurried across the grass to the dairy. The yard was mucky with red mud, the cows standing patiently in the rain. Inside, his father had turned the lights on against the gloom, and was kneeling, inspecting a cow's hoof. Saul started work, and as he moved the cattle through the stalls he thought of what might have been if Mae had pretended to everyone in the valley that Allie was his child. She could have, they would have believed her. Perhaps they would have married and built the cottage on his father's land, but it was more likely that they would have descended into arguments like that day in the milk bar when she had seemed like another person altogether.

His father came over and leaned against a post. 'How are you doing, son?'

'What do you mean?'

'It's that girl back in the valley isn't it? It's like young Mae's come back. I know she's been visiting you. Iris and I see her walking over to your place sometimes...'

Saul turned back to washing down a cow's udder.

His father leaned towards him. 'Are you listening?'

'I heard you.'

'I saw Julia today and she said to remind you about the girl's birthday dinner next week. I asked Julia why on earth you would be going to her birthday, and she said she didn't know. Just mind yourself, Saul. Mind yourself.'

Saul stood up and went to the far end of the shed and heaved a sack of barley onto his shoulder.

Working his body had been his only comfort after he found out Mae was having the balloon man's baby. Each day when his father went back to the house to eat lunch and rest for half an hour in the shade of the verandah, Saul had stayed out in the paddock, digging postholes for a new fence, letting the midday heat course through his veins. He wanted his sweat to slough the longing for Mae from his cells. He started avoiding people, despising them for agreeing that she was not good enough for him and that he was better off without her. At the last Hall dance he ever went to, an old school friend came to lean on the wall beside him and described the balloon man buying Mae a stick of fairy floss at the

Show. He had ignored his friend and concentrated instead on the dancers spinning past, churning up the hot air and trailing cigarette smoke and scent. A plump girl from down the valley kept asking him to dance. She had slipped easily into his arms, her perfume strong and perspiration shiny on her neck. They kissed outside and he nearly recoiled. Her lips were different to Mae's and she sucked on his tongue in a strange way. He wanted to say no, that she was doing it wrong, that he wanted Mae, then he found himself imagining that it was Mae that he was kissing and was suddenly aroused to think of her familiar mouth sliding beneath his. He fucked her up against the back wall of the hall, imagining Mae's body opening to his.

Afterwards, leaning against the rough boards, he smelt the girl's sour breath and felt her sweaty flesh under his hand. He turned and stumbled across the dark grass to the gate and headed down the road until the sounds of music from the hall faded and there was just the crunching of his shoes on the gravel. He walked all the way up the valley to Mae's place and waded through the foaming water of the little creek and climbed the bank, startling a group of cattle that staggered to their feet, calling out in fright. A baby's cry came from the house, a high, thin, mysterious sound. He wanted to go closer, to the source of the sound, but a light went on in the kitchen and the dogs started barking, so he turned back over the creek.

In the long paddock he started running and shut his eyes to the night air streaming past his skin. He was almost flying, running faster and faster, his chest aching with each breath, until he stumbled and his body slammed onto the hard ground. He had no breath and no way of breathing. Mae was in her house, with no idea that he was so close and that he had just given away his virginity to some girl whose name he didn't even know. He curled up and cried in the damp grass of her father's paddock.

chapter fifteen

Allie leaned toward the bathroom mirror and pinched her cheeks like her mother used to whenever she went out the front door. There were the sounds of people arriving, footsteps on the verandah and the door banging shut. Her great-grandmother's voice was loud in the living room, 'You need more gravel on your driveway Julia. Call Stan McGuire for a load, will you? Charge it to my account if you must. It's a quagmire.' Allie looked through a crack in the bathroom door. The old woman handed Julia a plate covered in tinfoil and then bent down to pick burrs from the brown stockings on her thin legs.

Julia frowned. 'I didn't ask you to bring anything, Grandma. I've prepared everything.'

'I always bring something, you know that.' She turned back to the door, 'Dan, Dan, did you bring the present from the car?'

A man threw open the back door and wiped his

boots vigorously on the door mat. He was tall and had bushy greying hair and a weathered face. Her mother's Uncle Dan. One of the four uncles.

'Where's Allie, Julia?' the old woman asked.

'She's getting ready, she won't be long.' Julia bustled out of her line of sight.

Headlights shone through the trees as a car came up the driveway. It would be him. Allie pulled off her dress, stepped into the bath and lay back, her eyes shut. She hadn't been to Saul's place for a few days—she had spent her time in the potting shed, going over what Mae had told her about him. Mae had even described the way she felt after they made love and how he had held her as they fell asleep in the forest. The heat of the bath was making Allie's head spin, her legs and feet seemed far in the distance, disconnected from her body. Her skin was flushing bright pink like Mae's always did in the bath.

'Allie?' It was Petal at the bathroom door. 'Can I come in?' She opened the door. 'Oh, you're still in the bath. Everyone's here.' She lifted the skirt of her long purple dress and sat on the toilet. 'It's beautiful, the china doll that Julia gave you. Saul's here. He wasn't sure if you still wanted him to come.'

'What do you mean?'

'He told me that you've been thinking he was your father. Is that what your mother told you?'

Allie stood up in the bath and grabbed a towel. She started drying herself roughly, rubbing hard at her tender skin.

Petal turned to flush the toilet. 'Oh. Don't be mad, sweetheart. I was over getting some milk from his dad and Saul told me what happened the other day. He's just worried about how you reacted.'

Allie wrapped the towel around herself and stepped out of the bath. 'Don't you think my mother would know? I mean wouldn't you have a pretty good idea?'

'Yeah, I'd have a pretty good idea, unless I was sleeping with two guys at once...'

Allie stared back at Petal.

Petal smiled. 'Remember you asked if he was married?'

'I know he's not.'

'He was married down in Tasmania. He worked for a jeweller and married the boss's daughter. They're separated but not divorced.'

'What's her name?'

'I don't know.' Petal came close behind her and reached over to pick up Julia's talcum powder from the shelf and smell it. 'So, what do you do at Saul's? I hear you've been going over there almost every day.'

'And what if I do?'

'Nothing if you do.' She raised her eyebrows. 'I was just curious what you get up to. He's a bit of a mystery, the old Saul. I thought you might have some light to shed on him.'

'He's not a mystery.'

'So, do you just hang out, or what?'

Allie shook her head. 'We talk.'

Petal rubbed the silky powder into Allie's back. 'Have you ever met your father?'

'No.' She turned to the mirror and dragged the comb through her long hair. Mae had suddenly stopped talking about the balloon man when Allie was about six. There were no more stories about the beautiful big

balloon or the handsome balloonist. No more promises
to take her to the Easter Show to find him.

Petal put the powder back on the shelf. 'Wouldn't
Julia know something?'

'Mae would know!' Allie's voice was loud. 'For God's
sake, she's the one who would know!' Allie combed her
hair straight down so it hung severely each side of her
face. She touched her flushed cheeks. She was a hollow
kewpie doll from the Show, cheap plastic that caves in
at a touch.

They sang happy birthday before they ate, the old
woman's quavering voice the loudest. Allie sat beside
Saul and watched his eyes flicking around the table as
he sang. She recalled Mae's forced smile when she once
stopped her mother in the middle of a story. 'But didn't
you say his eyes are brown like mine?' Mae's smile grew
wider, shining red lipstick stretching over her white
teeth. 'No, no, I didn't say that. They're blue. Blue and
green.' She was so sure that her stories would never be
put to the test.

'Lovely rich gravy, Julia,' said the old woman. 'I
taught both the girls to make gravy, Allie. Did your
mother make it for you?'

'Yes.' Every Sunday Mae stood at the stove in an
apron, her wooden spoon skating around the roasting
pan.

'And she cooked you up birthday dinners like this?
Made you a cake?'

'She got me a clown one year. He did cartwheels
down the back lane. Tom was supposed to pay for it
but he never turned up and she had an argument with

the clown in the kitchen.'

Saul smiled at her. 'So was the clown any good?'

'No. He was pretty hopeless.' She held his gaze and remembered the clown's sweaty wig on the kitchen table while he and Mae argued. She had woken in the middle of the night and heard the clown's voice and Mae's giggle as her mother let him out the front door. 'But Mae thought he wasn't so bad.'

Saul took a breath as if he were going to say something, then he picked up his fork to eat.

The old woman patted at her lips with a serviette. 'If we still had the old family farm we could have had a party for you there, dear. But it's not ours anymore. Barry Williams went up the other week to fix the pump for the new owners and told me that the place is a dreadful mess.' She nodded at Petal, 'So remind me where you fit into the picture. You're one of Julia's friends, are you? One of the new ones come up from the city?'

'I'm the one that camps here, on Julia's property.'

Dan laughed. 'I'm surprised you could find any clear ground to pitch a tent.'

'I'm in a caravan actually.'

'But there's rubbish everywhere, right? Weeds and rubbish trees all over the property.'

Julia spoke quietly. 'It's not rubbish, Dan. I'm letting the forest reclaim its land.'

'But why?' he leaned forward, his eyes wide.

'I know you don't understand. We've been through this before.'

'Try me, Julia.'

'It's a token effort to make up for what the family did to the valley.'

'No. No,' he laughed dryly. 'What you're doing is just like... it's like spitting in my father's face and your father's face. This is good land.' He poured more beer. 'Dad gave it to Bess and Jim to farm. Give it back to me and I'll manage it how Dad would have wanted. You stay in the house and I'll look after the farm.'

Julia's voice grew hard. 'Good land is it? Dad always said he and Mum were given the crappiest corner of Granddad's property.'

'Oh, really, Julia!' The old woman put down her glass with a bang.

'Well it's totally worthless now it's infested with weeds.' Dan pushed back in his chair.

'I guess it depends on your definition of "worthless," Danny. I might have a certain definition for what you left behind when you and Grandma sold up to the hobby farmers. Have you seen the erosion in your old paddock near Cobb's Corner?'

'Julia,' the old woman cut in, raising her voice over the rain that was growing heavier on the roof. 'Your father may not have been the world's best farmer but at least he kept his paddocks clean before the accident and even you did your best to keep the rubbish down while he was alive. What you are doing now is plain disrespectful.' She waved her arm, 'Just look at the place!'

Julia looked down at her plate and cut her meat into small pieces. Dan regarded her, a smile on his face.

Allie had been watching Saul, the way his eyes kept returning to her as the conversation eddied around them. She was still dizzy from the heat of the bath, sweat rolling down her skin under the loose dress.

He leaned towards her, his voice low. 'How're you

going?'

She whispered, 'She really did tell me that you did it.'

His face dropped and he shook his head. 'No. Honestly, no.'

'You're saying she's a liar?'

He took a deep breath. 'I think it's what she would have wished for.'

Allie spoke loudly, interrupting her grandmother, 'Did she tell all of you about the balloon man? Saul says everyone knew about the balloon man.'

There was silence around the table. Saul looked back at her, his expression unreadable.

'Yes,' the old woman sounded puzzled. 'If you mean that scoundrel from the Show. Yes, she told us. Why?'

'Allie…' Saul held her gaze and shook his head lightly.

Her great-grandmother wrinkled her brow. 'What are you talking about, Allie dear? Do you mean to say she didn't tell you about him?'

Petal poured wine into Allie's glass. 'It's your birthday, you're allowed.'

'She told me stuff.' Allie wanted Mae's stories laid out on the table. She wanted to shove the glasses and plates and platter of meat aside and lay the stories out and pull the threads of them apart in front of everyone, strand after strand, like a rug unravelling, the wool loosened until there was nothing left. The wine was sour on her tongue. 'She told me that no-one went to visit her in hospital when she had me. None of you. That's one of the things she told me.'

'She was only there for two days, love,' Dan said.

Julia put her knife and fork down. 'It wasn't… it

was in the middle of a huge flood, you know that. Mum and I couldn't get in. But Dad went to visit her. He stayed with the Carsons in town and went over to see her at the hospital the next day.'

'He did not!' Allie said.

Julia lifted her hands into the air and shrugged. 'He did, sweetheart. He wanted to take her back to the Carsons, because the hospital had been flooded, but she wouldn't go.'

Allie shook her head. 'Anyway, what about the rest of you?' She looked around the table, 'You could have gone.'

The old woman patted her serviette to her lips. 'I'll tell you why, my dear. The flood certainly made it difficult but the other thing is that she…shamed us. We could have sent her off to some school…some place where they take girls in trouble. But we let her stay here in the valley and we would have gone to visit her if she hadn't discharged herself from the hospital like a fool and hitched home in the rain. We couldn't pretend that everything was the way it should be. Nothing was the way it should have been, was it Saul?'

Saul shut his eyes.

Julia pushed back from the table. 'No, Grandma. There was never any talk of shame, not in this house and this is the one that mattered. For God's sake, what do you think you are saying…?' She gestured towards Allie.

'It affected the family all the way through the valley, Julia. I wouldn't expect you to remember and you wouldn't have been privy to the adult conversations. Allie knows it was nothing to do with her—all babies are born perfectly innocent and pure.'

Allie said, 'You know, she lay awake the whole night, waiting for someone to come. Anyone.' She looked at Saul, who had opened his eyes. 'Anyone.'

He shook his head.

Julia stood up and started clearing dishes away. 'It's not right what you are saying, Grandma. It's just not true.'

Dan passed Julia his plate. 'Mae did the wrong thing by Saul. Why would he go to visit her?'

Saul stood up and carried his plate to the sink. 'Thanks Dan, but I don't need you to speak for me.'

Dan raised his eyebrows and selected a toothpick from the jar on the table.

The old woman looked over at Julia and then back to Allie, her voice soft. 'It's better you know what really happened. But it's all over now, long gone.' She sat up straight and passed Julia the serving dishes.

'And no-one knows where he is, this balloon man?' said Allie.

'You don't want to find him, my dear. Not a fellow like that. Your family is here, right here.' The old woman leaned over and squeezed her hand, then got up and walked to the window. 'Dan, I'm worried about this rain, the town bridge could well go under. I think we'd better go.'

Saul stood beside Allie on the front verandah as they watched Julia walk the old woman out to the car with an umbrella.

'You know, it really was terrible, the storm, the flood when you were born,' he said. 'There's no way Julia or her mum could have got in. It's a miracle she and her father made it. They could have ended up halfway down the bloody creek. It happens, you know. Cars get carried away. People have drowned.' He leaned his elbows onto the railing, 'She wouldn't have wanted me to visit her anyway, even if I could have got through.'

'Oh yes, she would have.'

He looked at her and shook his head.

Here he was, this man she had spent years waiting for, the heat of his body just an arm's length away and nothing was like it was meant to be. Everything had started to go wrong, as if the world were thrown off its axis, the planet wobbling in the wrong orbit. She held her hands up in front of her and turned them back and forth. 'You and I have the same shape hands, different to Mae's.'

'We do, too.' He smiled. 'Your father must have hands like this. I don't know what Mae told you, I think it was what she would have preferred to have happened, you know. But there is no way that I am your father. There is absolutely no way.' He rested his head in his hands for a moment. 'I wish she was here. I wish she could clear things up.'

Julia was picking her way up the path under her umbrella, stopping to examine some bushes.

Allie spoke quickly, 'Why didn't you ever do it, then?'

Saul reached his hand out into the rain and turned his palm back and forth. 'She wanted to wait...' His voice was quiet. 'So we waited.'

Allie felt like all the blood in her body was draining away, out through her feet, between the cracks in the verandah boards and into the wet earth.

Julia walked up the steps and shook out the umbrella

as Petal appeared out of the rain, her wet hair flat to her head. Petal ran up the steps and grabbed Allie's arm. 'Come on. My present for you is down here.'

Allie let Petal take her down the path and through the gate, Petal's torch bobbing crazily, lighting up the streaking rain. She looked back at the verandah where Julia was holding the door open for Saul, who laughed at something Julia said as he stepped inside.

At the chook house, the birds were clucking and shuffling on their roost. Petal pulled her to one corner. 'Look.' She shone her torch on a small hen that turned its neat head to one side and blinked its eyes. 'It's for you. Your own bantam chook. Happy birthday.'

'Oh. Thank you.'

The hen fluffed its golden-red feathers and settled onto the perch. Allie sat on a wooden nesting box beside the hen, the dusty mealy smell of the chickens all around her. She pressed her fingers to the aching knot in her throat.

Petal sat beside her and they looked over to the house, at Saul and Julia framed in the kitchen window, steam clouding the glass as they washed up. Saul's hair was black and his shirt ruby red in the warm light. He nodded his head as he wiped the dishes, moving the tea towel slowly around and around a big white plate.

'She didn't want the guy from the Show to be the one,' Allie said. 'She wanted Saul. She didn't even try to find the balloon man. She didn't *want* to find him, right? What does that tell you?'

Petal looked at her in the faint light coming from the house, then reached across and squeezed Allie's knee.

The chickens around them clucked companionably,

feathers rustling as they shuffled and settled on their roosts.

'You know that clown?' Allie said. 'She fucked him. It's an easy way to pay bills, you know. Taxis… the local grocer.'

'It's okay, you know. It's okay that she did that.'

'You think so?' Allie shook her head, 'I saw you with a guy last night.'

'You did? You saw me with Billy?'

Allie nodded.

Petal laughed, 'I would have told him to be more dramatic if I'd known we had an audience. What were you doing outside my van?'

Allie shrugged, 'Walking.' She watched Saul wiping a wine glass, carefully twisting the tea towel into the bowl of the glass. 'He says they never had sex.' She picked up a piece of straw from the floor. 'When did you first have sex?'

'When I was fifteen. Your age. With a friend of my brother's, a surfer.' Petal touched a finger to her tongue. 'His skin tasted like salt. I found out later that my brother was watching through the window. I think he set it up.'

'She told me they did it. But she told me a lot of things.' Allie remembered sitting on the front step for hours. Sometimes Mae would come and sit behind her and when a man walked up the street, Mae would go quiet and examine him, then lean close and say, 'No.' Occasionally she would pause, and wait, letting him get closer and closer. Allie would hold her breath, waiting for him to see them, preparing to meet the First Love, until Mae said, 'No. Not him either, sweetheart.'

In the darkness of the chook house, Allie pressed her fists hard against her eyes. It was as if the burning tears were forcing their way out through the very skin around her eyes.

chapter sixteen

Julia passed Saul a soapy dish. 'I hope you were categorically clear that you're not her father?'

He grimaced. 'Julia, I was clear, I was absolutely clear. I don't know where she got the idea. No, I do know. I'd forgotten what Mae was like.'

'You have no idea it was Mae. It could just be a fantasy in Allie's head.'

'You think so?'

Julia scrubbed at a saucepan with steel wool. 'I don't want you spending so much time with her, Saul. She's been visiting you almost every day.'

'What is this about?'

'This is about the fact that you're not her father and you're too old to be her friend.'

He put the tea towel down on the bench. 'That's not your decision to make Julia.'

'Oh, really?'

'Yes, really.'

'She's been spying on you, you know.'

'Yes, I know. She's fifteen, Julia. Not a little kid. You don't have to breathe down her neck. Remember Mae at that age? Don't smother her.'

'She's not Mae and I'm sick of everyone saying it. She's nothing like Mae! She hardly talks, I have no idea what's going on…'

'For God's sake, she's in grief! When my mother died I was in a dream for months.'

'She's not Mae! Just stop thinking that.'

'I'm not thinking that. I'm saying she's a young adult and you'll drive her away if you treat her like a child.'

Julia crashed the pan down on the sink. 'I do not treat her like a child!'

'Okay, okay… How about a cuppa? God, I need a cuppa after that dinner-table discussion. I'd forgotten what an arsehole Dan is.'

Julia was silent, her hands in the soapy water.

He reached for another plate. 'How are your trees going?'

'Don't patronise me, Saul.'

He sighed. 'Fine. That's fine, Julia. I've got to go.'

He walked to the front door, Julia behind him. A car's lights reversed into the driveway, then turned back down the road the way it came.

'Oh, shit,' he said.

'So, both bridges… You can stay here. It'll be down in the morning.'

He called his dog in from the rain. 'I'll sleep on the couch.'

'No. Sleep in my bed and I'll sleep in with Allie. There are two beds in there.' She turned and went inside.

Saul lay awake in Julia's bed. The rain sounded hollow on the unfamiliar tin roof. He turned on the bedside lamp and from the high brass bed looked around the room at the piles of papers and the dusty wooden dresser. The leak bucket was almost full, brimming with clear still water and shimmering with each drip.

He turned in bed, pulling the sheet around him and thought of Mae's old man sleeping in this very bed, fucking here, dying here. Saul had left for Tasmania soon after Mae had gone. He'd never seen her father after the accident and it was hard for him to imagine the big man crumpled and weak. He didn't feel any satisfaction to be lying in the man's bed, to be alive when he was dead. Instead it felt like the bastard was still watching him.

Allie's questions had reminded him of the incredible frustration and delight of exploring Mae's body. He realised now how generous she had been in opening her body to his curiosity. She had been a mystery unfolding to him, the smell of her, the soft folds of skin, the slippery eggwhite of her arousal. Except that she would never let him inside where he wanted to be.

He held his hands up in front of him. It was just a crazy fluke that Allie's were like his. When he was a boy, he wished for hands like his father's—muscular, with thick fingers and broad palms. Farmer's hands. He could recall even the shape of the moons on his father's fingernails and his crooked left index finger. When Saul had mumps as a boy, his father had sat up all night

sponging him with a damp washer, while outside the
rain thundered down. 'There you go,' his father's voice
had been barely audible over the noise of the rain. 'It's
okay, little man. It's okay.' His hands were gentle even
as Saul called out for his mother who was not long dead.
He was convinced she was in the next room, hiding
from him, withholding herself. 'Mummy,' he called out.
'Where are you? Go away, Dad.' And still his father had
sat beside him, fanning him with an old Japanese paper
fan and in the pre-dawn carrying him through the rain
to the dairy and laying him, wrapped in his bedclothes,
on a row of hay bales. Saul had listened to the comfortable,
familiar sounds of the cows and pulled the blankets
around him—the fever finally gone—and watched his
father working with those strong broad hands.

He got out of Julia's bed and walked through the
dark house for a smoke on the verandah. He passed the
shut door of Allie's bedroom and wondered if she slept
like Mae, with her eyes disconcertingly half-open. His
dog greeted him, shivering with pleasure, then he saw
Julia sitting in the dark on one of the cane chairs. She
sat very still and didn't look up.

'Hi.' He felt awkward after their earlier discussion
and wished he'd gone to the other verandah but sat
down beside her and started to roll a cigarette.

She spoke abruptly. 'I can see why she would want
you to be her father. I mean, what's the other option?
Some unknown, untraceable guy who used to drag a
balloon around with the Show.'

'Is he really untraceable? I'll help her find him.
I mean, there must be some way to track him down.'

'He's untraceable.' She was silent. 'He's probably

running a pub in some town somewhere now, or...
I don't know.'

In the darkness he felt bold. 'How did she die, Julia?'

'Mae drowned.'

'Yes, but I also heard...'

'What?'

'I just want to know if there's more to it.'

Her voice was tight. 'Why do you need to know?'

He shrugged and lit his cigarette, the flame lighting
up his and Julia's legs stretched out in front of them,
identically crossed at the ankle.

'I don't really know, Saul, but the police are convinced
it was intentional.'

'And how are they convinced of that?'

She pulled her bare feet up onto the seat, and hugged
her knees to her chest. 'This man saw her, you know.
He was riding on the last ferry out near the Heads and
looked down and saw a mermaid floating on the swell.
The most beautiful woman he had ever seen, he said.
A naked woman with long dark hair over her shoulders
out in the middle of the bloody harbour. Apparently
she smiled at him and then dived down and disappeared
into the water.'

'What the hell was she doing out there?'

Julia stood up and reached her hand out into the
rain, spattering it in on him. 'He dived in after her, can
you believe? I read his statement, the policeman showed
me. This guy jumped off the ferry deck after her. It
must have been dark as hell and he started looking for
her, diving down, hoping to grab an ankle or a hand,
but nothing. Just her little dinghy left floating out there.'

'She could swim anywhere, you know that as well

as anyone. She would never drown by accident.'

'They're saying it wasn't an accident. No accident, Saul.' Julia wiped her hands on her pants and walked inside the house.

He followed her. 'But how do the police figure it was intentional just because she dived down?'

She turned and looked at him for a moment before replying, her voice a whisper, 'Like you say, she was a brilliant swimmer... and she phoned me before she went out.'

'That night?'

She nodded and stroked the wood of the dining table.

'What did she say?'

'That she was calling in her debts and I must get on the next train to Sydney and come straight to the house. And when I asked why, why should I get on a bloody train now, long after I'd given up waiting for her to ask me to come, she just said, "Please, please." And when I spoke again she'd gone.' She tapped the table. 'I should have called someone. I could have called and woken Allie or called the police... I could have called someone but I hung up the phone and went back to bed. So, that's the truth. I might have saved her and I decided not to.'

'How were you to know? How could anyone expect... What did she mean "calling in her debts"?'

'There are debts that run both ways between Mae and me.' She picked up a torch by the front door and turned to look back at him. 'I'm going out to check on the trees.'

He followed her onto the verandah. 'Hang on, Julia.

Does Allie know how Mae died?'

'No.'

'You're going to tell her, right?'

'I'm trying to find the right words. If you think of them, Saul, feel free to let me know.'

'I can't believe she would do it deliberately, leaving Allie all alone. I don't believe it.'

Julia walked down the steps. 'She didn't leave her alone, Saul. She left her to me.'

He watched her disappear into the darkness then threw his cigarette out into rain, the glowing red tip extinguished in a second as it arced through the air.

chapter seventeen

Saul's dog was nuzzling Allie, its wet nose nudging her where she was curled on the hard boards, her back to the rain driving in under the verandah roof. Mae's skin would be silvery scales now, seaweed and fish tangled in her hair. When Allie heard Julia telling Saul the story, she could picture the man diving from the ferry, the fool not knowing Mae was long gone, fast and lithe through the water with her muscular mermaid's tail. And while he was thrashing about looking for her, while the ferry was slowing and turning, there must have been the moment that Mae looked up at the trail of bubbles rising through the thick black water and realised that it was too late, that the surface was too far away and she had gone too deep. And as she tried to swim back up through the cold water, her breath running out, she would have thought of Allie.

She woke again at daybreak. The dog was gone and she sat up, damp and aching. Inside, Julia was asleep on the lounge, her arms flung above her head, one breast half spilling from her muddy dress. She looked down at her aunt's sleep-soft face for evidence of last night's words, expecting to see bruising on Julia's skin or a rent in her translucent eyelids.

She had been asleep on the outside day bed when Saul and Julia's voices woke her. For a while their voices merged with the rain and she started to drift back to sleep, until Julia's words cut though the darkness, every syllable distinct. After they went inside she found herself down on the verandah boards, her cheek pressing hard onto the wood. It was as if a great weight was crushing her, tons of black water squeezing the breath from her.

Saul's car was gone and the rain was washing away the last of the paw prints and boot marks in the mud by the gate. She stood in the misty rain and looked up to the escarpment, where great white plumes of water sprayed out from the waterfall. Mae had pointed it out to her when they visited and told her that she used to go up and stand on the very edge, looking down to where the water exploded on the rocks at the bottom. She had once read Allie an article from a *Reader's Digest* about some kind of force exerted at the edge of cliffs that had been known to draw people over against their will.

It took her hours to get up there. She dug her fingers into the decaying leaves to climb the steep hill, prickly vines grabbing at her, sweat stinging her scratched skin. The roaring of the waterfall faded in and out as she pushed through the dense growth. She reached the top and came out onto a broad rock shelf where the water ran in a swirling frenzy, foaming through potholes and pools, rushing over the slick dark ribbon of rock. As it flung itself off the edge, the water seemed to slow and drift, each drop frozen in its own free fall.

She didn't believe Mae's story about the bullocks anymore. She didn't believe that a team of bullocks would be up there at the head of the waterfall, crossing with a load of timber. How many times had Mae described them struggling for a grip on the smooth rock, hooves scrabbling as the water swept them to the edge. She said they sailed out into mid-air with the rushing water, twisting and tangling in their traces, eyes wide with terror, falling slowly, silently, as graceful as the water. Allie used to picture them, the bullocky on the bank urging them on, shouting and cracking the whip as they slipped, their wagon skewing behind them, the load of logs loosening and somersaulting after them. Mae had let her believe the bullock story. She had just sat there on Allie's bed and let her cry for them and ask again how desperately the bullock drivers tried to unhitch the wagon and save the animals.

She stood on the edge of the cliff, where gusts of wind blew the water mist back and the rain pelted her until everything was water, running down her face, gluing her eyelashes together and sliding between her lips.

The water slipped over the edge so easily, it glided like glass over the lip of rock. She was sure that Mae had stood there and wondered what it would be like to take a step, an everyday step out into the air.

How long had her mother waited at Allie's door before she went down to the harbour that night? How long had she stood there, in the dark hallway, listening to her breathe, like she did when Allie was a baby? In the morning Allie had woken to the banging on the front door and from her bed saw Tom coming down the stairs, buttoning his pants. He had opened the door and there was the rumbling of male voices. She remembered Tom's singlet was nubbly on her skin where he crushed her against him and she noticed that his wrist was pale where his watch normally sat. He shuddered against her and she didn't realise until later that he was crying. The fisherman standing at the front door beside the policeman had smiled at her, a fleeting smile until he looked away and smoothed his pants. She had fixed her eyes over the man's head, on the patch of sky framed in the doorway, an early morning pale blue. She had thought that if the sun was coming up as usual, everything would be okay. She had convinced herself that things must be all right if the sun was shining over the whole wide city.

Allie found the path back down from the escarpment and started running, barely staying upright, her feet sinking into the leaf litter. It was as if she were just staying ahead of a chasm opening in the ground behind her. At the bottom of the valley she followed the small flooded creek towards Saul's place, and stepped from rock to deep silty mud, struggling through sodden banks of reeds. The curves in the creek were flooded over, the water flowing swift and brown, fence posts and tree trunks slicing the satiny surface. She shut her eyes to the rain. Rain and mud. That's all there was in the end. Ashes to dust to dirt to mud. Mae was everywhere. She was the red mud being washed down into the swollen creek, her mother slipping through her fingers again.

She lay on his back verandah and waited. When she heard his car pulling up and the front door banging shut, she stood up and let her feet take her to him. He gave her a dry T-shirt and shorts and pulled the sticky black leeches from her ankles. He washed her scratches, the cotton wool and warm water like balm on her skin, bloody water trickling down her leg into a bowl. He carefully stretched a Band-Aid over the cut on her calf.

Lightning and thunder rolled around the valley and there was the seamless sound of the rain, on and on, filling every crevice in the room, stopping every thought before it began. His hair was soaking wet and she could see through the strands of black to his pale scalp. One curling slick of hair brushed his ear, a drop of water quivering at its tip.

When she leaned forward and kissed him, he pulled back for a second, then there was the soft muscle of his lips moving against hers, his whiskers scratching her chin and his hand cupping the side of her head.

chapter eighteen

Julia sat on the couch in the dim light of her living room, for the first time afraid that the thin layer of roofing tin between her and the rain would not be enough.

Allie had been gone for hours. Julia had woken to an empty house, her own bed neatly made, Allie's not slept in. She had walked down the road in the rain and stood by the side of the raging creek. It was just passable and she could see the tracks of Saul's tyres in the mud on the other side.

She hated how her words had spilled over Saul last night, looking for some absolution that could never be given, least of all by him. The night that Mae telephoned her, Julia had hung up the phone and gone back to bed and simply waited. It seemed she had spent years of her life lying in bed, waiting. Waiting for Mae to sneak back in from Saul's, waiting for the baby to come, waiting

for Mae to contact her, waiting for her father to die.
Waiting for the forest to consume her.

There was a loud noise at the verandah door. A pigeon
was fluttering wildly against the glass, panicking in the
storm. She went out onto the verandah and shooed the
bird back out into the wind and rain. After her father
died, Neal would come to the door at dusk. He would
appear without a sound, used to moving silently after
years of living in the forest, and he would wipe his feet
and knock, an incongruous sight with his long beard
and hand raised, tapping formally on the door. She
missed the sense that he was just out there in the forest,
only a ten-minute walk away. He showed her the cave
the first time they made love. She had followed him in
silence along the forest track, just the crackling of the
heated bush around them and small birds flitting though
the undergrowth. They climbed hundreds of metres up
a steep slope to the cave, where snakes had left their
sinuous trails on the sandy floor and swallows peered
from small mud nests. They sat and looked out at the
sea of trees below. The dark rainforest and bright green
camphors. For hours it seemed they sat there, the sounds
of birds and distant farm machinery rising from the
valley. He had unbuttoned her shirt as if he had never
seen buttons, as if he were figuring out how to work
them. His body over hers had been so big, his broad
square shoulders and muscular arms. The sand shifted
under her and the breeze coming up from the valley
brushed against her bare skin.

She grabbed her raincoat from its hook and hurried
down the steps into the house paddock. Two days ago
she had planted a silky oak right into the faint furrow

where her father's tractor had rolled. Her mother had got there first and dragged him across to the house, leaving a trail of blood in the grass and dirt. Julia remembered standing on the verandah looking down at him while her mother called up to her and Mae to help carry him to the car. He had looked like a snail crushed on the cement path, broken and oozing juice.

She stood in the paddock and turned in a slow circle, listening. The roaring of the creek echoed around the valley as if it were flowing right by the house. There was something frighteningly relentless about the way the creek was rising this time, the water stronger and rougher than it had been for years.

Two nights before Allie was born, Julia and Mae had lain in their beds, listening to the boulders crashing down at the creek. Mae was curled on her side and had lifted her nightdress so Julia could lay her hand on the taut warm skin and feel the shape of the baby underneath. That warmth, that quickening, was Allie.

Julia hadn't touched Mae's belly before, horrified by the way it had stretched and stretched until it seemed her skin would split. Everything at home seemed normal, the milking went on every day and preparations for Christmas had started but in the midst of it all there was Mae's belly swelling grotesquely, ignored by everyone.

When Mae's contractions started in the middle of the night, her mother came into their room and sat on Mae's bed. 'It's okay. This is normal, sweetheart.'

Mae's face was pale. 'But how am I going to get to the hospital?'

'The flood waters are going down. You won't have the baby yet, that's quite a few hours off, I'd say. Just try and get some rest.'

Mae had walked around the house through the night. She wouldn't sit. She wouldn't take the cups of tea her mother offered. Dawn came and their father called Julia out to the bottom paddocks to help move the cattle up to the higher ground. She hated it, slipping in the mud and manure, cows' tails flicking her with watery shit.

Mae's contractions came and went all morning and she drifted in and out of sleep. After lunch their mother sent Julia down to the creek to check the water level, even though they all knew that with the rain so heavy there was no way it would have dropped.

Julia woke the second night to Mae screaming, 'Get me the doctor!' Mae and her mother were in the kitchen, the lights blazing on Mae where she leaned her elbows on the table, retching. Her mother was calmly stroking Mae's back until Mae started sobbing that something was wrong with the baby. 'It's dying, I can feel it. It's dying. It's not going to come out.'

Her mother looked up at Julia. 'Go and get your raincoat, quick.'

Julia was pulling her coat down when her father came in from checking on the cattle. He saw Mae curled on the floor and walked right into the house in his gumboots, red mud on the lino. He bent down and picked her up. 'Right, I'm driving her in.'

'You won't get over the town bridge. Don't even try.' Her mother took hold of his elbow but he brushed her off and carried Mae through the rain to the truck.

Julia and her mother stood on the verandah watching the tail-lights disappear. Her mother's voice was flat. 'Go to bed Julia. Get some sleep.'

Julia was standing by the little silky oak sapling when she heard the tree fall. It began like a distant gunshot, piercing the sound of the rain and the creek. Then came the long dull roaring of the tree ripping through the forest canopy, tearing down other trees and vines. On her walks Julia had seen the massive trees lying in the forest, shattered limbs all around and a bright gaping hole in the canopy above.

Petal came running up the dark paddock not even two minutes later, barefoot and eyes wild. She grabbed hold of Julia's arm, her hands cold. 'A tree smashed my van, a great fucking trunk right through the middle of it.'

Julia looked across to the wall of forest and felt a wash of fear.

'I pissed myself. I nearly died. And now everything is getting soaked, all my clothes and books.'

She followed Petal to the van. Lightning showed flashes of metal folded and crumpled under the pale tree trunk.

Petal pulled on Julia's arm, 'Come and help me get my stuff.'

Julia shook her head. 'Not now. Not in a storm. Not after a tree has fallen.' She could hear how high and thin her voice was. 'There are others it will have destabilised. They could fall too.' She started walking back to the house, wishing she were already safely inside.

'Nooo Julia. Come and help me!' Petal was right behind her.

Julia climbed the stairs and went straight into the

bathroom. 'I'm running you a bath,' she called to Petal. She had to strike the match three times before it took and as she held the tiny flame to the woodchips in the heater, she remembered Mae striking match after match in their cubby hole at the top shed, letting the flame go right down to her finger and thumb, the smell of burning flesh in the air.

chapter nineteen

The moment that his skin touched hers, it was as if she knew it already, like she was recalling it from some other time, the air moving by her skin as he carried her down the hallway, the sheets soft under her, his lips on her, in her. She tasted him and already knew the warm saltiness. At last she was inside the experience she had been outside of for so long. She could taste his tongue, like rain, like blood, inside her head. He was inside her.

She kept her eyes shut, to better feel every fold of the sheet he had spread over her and to hear the faint sounds of him moving through the house, turning a tap on, clinking a glass, speaking to his dog. There was still the trace of his hands on her body, where his fingers had pressed into her, where his hair had brushed her shoulder. She could taste his warm breath and smell him. She pulled the sheet over her shoulder against the rain spitting in through the open window. The breeze

moved across her skin like cool water. The currents must
have been so gentle, cradling the little Islander girl as
she floated out to sea, the fish all around her, the tiny
phosphorescent fish swimming in the tangle of her long
hair as if it were seaweed, brushing against her with
their silken scales. The sailor had cradled the little girl
on his lap all the way back to the Navy ship, holding
her tight against him, in case she was a dream.

She woke to Saul sitting on the bed beside her. He
was dressed in his work clothes and had his raincoat in
his hand. 'Hey, Allie. I've got to go up to Dad's. You'd
better get home. There's a huge bank of clouds coming
down the valley. Take care crossing Little Banana Creek.'
He smiled and rested his hand on her hip for a moment
and then he was gone before she was awake enough to
find words. She curled back into his soft bed, waiting
for the storm. It came in a rattling blast of wind, then
she dressed and moved out into it, lifting her face to
the stinging rain.

The boulders at the little creek were already underwater. There was no way across so she turned and pushed
back through the dripping bush to the road.

Halfway home Julia's car appeared in the distance.
Allie stood and waited for her.

Julia leaned over to open the door. 'Get in. I didn't
know where you were.' She carefully turned the car
around on the narrow road. 'What are you wearing'?

'Saul's clothes. Mine are at his place.'

'Really.' Julia's voice was dry. 'You don't know how
crazy it is to go out in a storm like this. And Saul
obviously didn't bother to tell you. Petal's van is smashed
by a tree.'

'Is she okay?'

'Yeah. She's at home, making dinner.'

Allie looked up at the silvery gums along the road. She couldn't imagine them crashing down. They were still and serene in the grey light, as unchanging as the falling rain.

Julia slowly steered the car into the muddy water rushing over the causeway. It looked deep to Allie and she felt the water pulling at the car as Julia drove across, the engine churning, a deep wake behind them.

Petal's clothes were strung around the house, bright lace hanging from the rope across the living room, satiny slips and skirts on the back of dining chairs. She called to Allie from the kitchen, 'I rescued some stuff, even though Miss Julia, the logger's granddaughter, forbade me.'

Allie and Petal ate scrambled eggs on their laps in the bedroom, a candle on the floor between them, while Julia was outside with a torch, throwing bricks onto the tin roof of the potting shed and wrestling plastic guards around the trees she had planted that day.

Allie put her plate down and curled onto the hard mattress, her body aching. Mae had said that the young American sailor wept as he made love to her. Allie could imagine crying while Saul moved over her, the heat of his breath on her cheek.

Petal lay back and put her legs up the wall. 'You know, after the tree fell, it groaned, this… sound came from inside it. Julia says they feel pain, that all plants hurt when we kill them. It was like a huge body, a massive fucking corpse lying on top of my poor van.' She slid her legs down the plaster and rolled over to face Allie. 'You were at Saul's all day, huh?'

'No, I went up to the waterfall first.' He might be back at his house by now, standing in his room, looking for the imprint of her body on the sheets. She reached under the bed for the wire face and lay back, tracing the lines of the mouth.

'That's one of Saul's!'

'Yeah.' The wire was smooth under her finger.

'She doesn't like you seeing him, you know. She was steaming around the house before she went to get you. Why does it rile her up so bad?'

'She's jealous.'

Petal raised her eyebrows, 'Jealous? Is this another one of your theories?'

Allie shrugged her shoulders. 'Tell me how you felt after the first time you had sex, with your brother's friend.'

Petal let out a long breath, 'Ohhhh...' She raised herself up onto one arm. 'Bloody hell... is that what's been going on? You and Saul?'

'That's not what I meant!'

'So what did he say to get to you, the crafty devil?'

'It's not like that. You don't understand.' She rolled over, her back to Petal. She wished she were in his bed, not here with the windows rattling in their frames and branches worrying the roof. She wished that he had kissed her goodbye.

Petal came to kneel beside her bed and the candle threw her wavering shadow onto the wall. 'Hey, don't pout. It's fine by me. Why should I have a problem with it? I wouldn't tell anyone else about it, though, if I were you. You know what the valley's like. They won't think well of you or him for it. By the way, I found out a bit more for you. His wife's name is Freya. Danish name. But they're well and truly over. Just thought you'd like to know.' She walked out, quietly pulling the door closed behind her.

chapter twenty

Saul leaned against the cow's warm flank. All afternoon he had a worming feeling in his guts whenever he remembered being with her. In the seconds before he came, he'd had a moment of clarity. He had seen her beneath him, and seen in her pale slender body every way she was not like Mae. Oh Christ what was he doing? Even as he tried to push himself off her, his body had surged forward and he clumsily pulled out, spilling into his hand, onto the sheets, onto her skin. He had wanted to get up, to lurch away from the bed, but there he was, leaning on one hand, suspended in shame and disbelief. Had he really pushed his cock into Mae's baby? Oh God.

He turned the dairy lights on and shovelled cow pats out into the dark rain then hosed down the concrete floor. He focused on the sensation of his muscles sliding over his bones, the sensation of honest work, of doing the right thing. He pulled the hood of his raincoat over his head and jogged down to the house. On the verandah he could smell dinner. Iris had come up through the rain to tell him she was keeping a plate warm for him. He called in the door, 'I'm off. I'm not hungry, thanks anyway. See you tomorrow!' He ran down the stairs before they could urge him in.

Walking away from the golden light of the farmhouse into the darkening bush, he couldn't help sinking into that part of him that wanted to remember the feel of Allie's body. And Mae's body. Their flesh, their softness, their hair. He leaned against a tree and masturbated into the darkness, feeling sick.

At his house there were car headlights shining across the lawn and a figure standing on the verandah. It couldn't be Allie, she didn't drive. He stood in the dark of the forest path, trying to see who it was. He didn't want a visitor, but started crossing the clearing, his torch lighting the way.

Julia marched over the grass to him, shouting, 'You bastard. You sleazy bastard. You and your compassion bullshit.'

He shut his eyes against her face that was red and contorted in the torchlight. There was a great thunderclap and flash of lightning. 'Come inside.' He grabbed her arm.

She wrenched her arm from him. 'Don't touch me. Don't fucking touch me, Saul Philips.'

The thunder came again, loud and close. He walked past her and up the verandah steps.

'What the hell were you thinking?' She was right behind him. 'You never got to do her mother, so you thought you'd get the daughter, eh? Righting old wrongs?' They stood facing each other on the dark verandah, her chest heaving and her hair hanging in dripping cat-tails.

'I wasn't thinking, Julia. That was the problem.' He stepped inside and flicked the light switch on and off. 'Oh shit.' He pulled down a kerosene lamp from the shelf and dried his hands on a towel before striking a match and lighting it.

She sat heavily into an armchair. 'So you actually did it?'

The dog scurried in the door and flattened itself to the floor near Saul's feet.

'You know what, Julia? You don't need to get involved. You're right, it was a mistake and I'll sort it out with her.' He adjusted the wick on the lamp. 'Actually it's none of your bloody business, just as it's none of your business whether I slept with your sister or not.'

She spoke quietly, 'I want you to stay away from her, Saul. No-one took care of Mae and I'm sure as hell not going to let the same thing happen to her daughter.' She tilted her head to one side. 'You must have forgotten there's such a thing as an age of consent in this country.'

'Heavy guns, huh?' He turned away from her and started towards his bedroom, 'Fine, Julia. Let yourself out.'

She stood up as his phone rang.

It was his father. 'Is your power out, Saul?'

'Yeah.'

'Was that Julia driving by like a maniac a little while ago?'

'Yep. It was.'

'She won't be getting back across. The bridge's well and truly under. The old weir up at Nilsson's just breached. Just thought she'd like to know.'

'Oh. Thanks, Dad. See ya.' He turned to Julia where she stood by the door. 'Why the hell did you come across if it was so high? It's gone under again.'

She stared at him and shook her head.

They sat across from each other in the dark, the kero lamp glowing on the coffee table between them.

'Were you going to do it again?' she said. 'If I hadn't found out, would you have had another go?'

He took a deep breath. He was empty of words, empty of any desire to placate Julia. He shook his head. 'No, I wasn't. You make it sound so... I was planning to talk to her about it. I was going to take care of it, Julia. How was she when she told you? You make it sound like she's upset.'

Julia picked at her fingers. 'She didn't tell me. She told Petal.' She lay down on his couch, punching a cushion under her head and closing her eyes.

Saul leaned his head back and looked up at the shadowy mobiles hanging from the ceiling. He wanted to lie down on his bed and sleep but was frozen in the armchair. If only he had pushed Allie away and held her at arm's length, arms strong and firm. He had thought of pulling back, but only for a second. His father was right, he was losing it.

In the moments when the rain eased, he could hear how loud the creek was. Nilsson's stone weir had never broken before. It had been built years earlier to create a bigger waterhole. All the valley kids learned to swim in that waterhole, old Mr Nilsson standing at the end by the rough cement diving blocks, a stopwatch in his hand. Normally Saul loved hearing that the creek had gone under, he had always liked the idea of being cut off from the rest of the world. When he was about five, he and his parents had been stranded for a night between two crossings. He only had wisps of memory—his father writing their names on the fogged-up car windows and his mother tipping her head back to eat a sliver of bottled peach. His parents had laid their seats back and he curled on the back seat, cocooned in his mother's soft cardigan, listening to the creek and his parents murmuring while he sucked the last of the sugar syrup from his fingers. They stayed there until just before dawn when the creek dropped enough for them to drive across.

He woke with a start. The rain had stopped and everything was quiet, just the sound of water dripping. Julia was curled on the sofa, her back to him. He picked up the lamp and walked quietly down the hall to his bedroom. He was unbuckling his belt when Julia's voice came from behind him.

'So this is where you did it?' Her voice was quiet and when he turned to look at her where she stood in the doorway, he was surprised by the sadness on her face.

He just wanted to be alone, to stretch out and sleep. 'Give it a rest, Julia.'

'You think it's a little thing? Just something to brush off?'

'No.' He sat down on the edge of his bed. 'I don't think it's a little thing but you know... I don't think it's the end of the world.'

'So what would the end of the world be?'

He looked up at her standing in his door, her clothes crumpled and long hair mussed. 'I'm tired, Julia. I don't understand.'

'The end of the world, Saul?' She slid down and sat on the floor. 'I used to pray you knew as well and were planning to do something. Or I'd pray that I imagined it, for a while I even convinced myself I didn't see anything.'

'See what?'

She didn't look at him as she spoke. 'I just went down to get some milk for Mum. I only went down for a jug of milk. The dairy was empty, just all the cows there and the machine thumping away, and I could have helped myself, but there was all that hygiene stuff and I knew he'd belt me if I messed it up, so I went to look for him. And even before I saw… I thought something was wrong. There was that sound, a kind of rustling and a groan. I thought… you know… somehow I thought that one of the dogs had died… had got poisoned and was writhing in the hay, like that one we found that ate bait. There was that noise. So I went in to see… I saw her first, her eyes, her head shaking, jerking. Dad was… fucking her. And when he saw me he kept going… can you believe… he kept going and ordered me into the dairy. And I went in to where all the cows were eating their barley, the machines sucking away, and then he came in and got the milk for me and he must have known I wouldn't say anything, he just measured the milk out. And I was listening for Mae, waiting to see her come in, as if it were all not true. I just walked back up to Mum at the house like an ordinary morning. I left her down there and I never said a word. It was like I just erased it from my mind. It's not that I forgot it… I just didn't remember,' she searched his face, '… and the worst thing is that he knew I wouldn't do anything.'

'Oh God, Mae.' Saul lit a cigarette, his hand shaking around the flame. He kept the match burning, to catch its faint warmth, to ease the vein of cold that snaked through his body. He pulled his knees up. Not the old man with Mae, not the old prick's prick. He shook his head. 'I didn't know, Julia. I had no idea.'

She nodded, 'I know.'

Saul pulled on his cigarette as a terrible sadness washed over him. 'The balloon man?'

'No. She went up in his balloon, that's all. I was with her all day, when we went up in the balloon and he tried to chat her up. She thought he was a joke. A skinny old guy with greasy black hair.' Her voice shook. 'He went along with her story, my dad did. Do you remember? How he wanted to track him down? He wanted to make the guy take responsibility.'

'I remember.' He pressed his fingers hard onto his shut eyelids. It was as if some crazy movie was running in his head—images of Mae, smiling up at him as he undressed her, turning her head away and closing her eyes when he pressured her again to let him make love to her. Mae across the table from him in Sydney, 'I'm not good enough for you, Saul. Go and find yourself a good wife.'

Julia had gone out onto the verandah and was looking out to the forest. She seemed so fragile standing there in the darkness. He remembered how small and nervous she was as a kid and thought of her carrying around the image of what she had seen. He curled up on his bed and wished he could weep for Mae. He curled up and prayed for sleep.

chapter twenty-one

Petal shook her awake. 'Look, the flood's coming up to the house.'

They stood at the bedroom window watching the lightning illuminate the great sheet of water creeping up the paddocks.

Petal said, 'It flows really fast underneath the surface, you know. I waded out into the last flood and it nearly took me away. It'll be ripping all her poor little trees out.'

'Where is she?'

Petal shrugged. 'I think she went to Saul's.'

'You told her!'

'Don't you think she could figure it out on her own?'

Allie walked away from Petal into the dark kitchen. 'I told you not to tell her.' She looked out the window. A white flash lit up the front garden. Julia's car was gone. Allie wondered whether he would describe to Julia how he had lifted her up to him, his hands spanning her back. Would he tell her the minute sensations of her skin under his fingertips?

Petal came up behind her, cupping her hand around a candle flame, her fingers glowing pink. 'What would Mae think of you and him?'

'Don't call her Mae. You don't even know her.'

'But what would she think?'

'She knows how gentle he is. She'd be glad.'

'She'd be glad?'

Allie nodded.

Petal put the candle down on the table. 'Even if she had… you know… a free attitude to sex, I don't think she'd be happy about you doing it with a man twice your age.'

'What do you mean a free attitude to sex?'

'Well, you told me about the clown and the grocer.'

Allie gritted her teeth against the memory of strange footsteps down the stairs late at night.

She looked out the window, waiting for another lightning flash. She pressed her nose to the cool glass. 'Plenty of men wanted to. They used to come around, knocking on the door. She'd send me down to tell them to go away.' Tom had been almost gentle in the way he gripped her arms and moved her to one side of the stairs.

The rain struck the glass so hard she was afraid it would break. If she had her dinghy they could moor it to the verandah in case the house went right under. Mae would be outside in weather like this, naked on the roof, arms spread to the sky, the rain like needles on her bare skin. After it ended with Tom, after that trip down south, she used to go out onto the roof every night. She would climb out the bedroom window, her bare feet gripping the sloping corrugated iron, and lean back against the painted brick wall and look out over the city. Sometimes Allie would get up in the middle of the night to go outside to the toilet and in the faint street light she could see her mother still up there, arms wrapped around her bent knees.

Allie opened the back door and Petal yelled across the room, 'Shut the door, it's a bloody gale.'

She stepped outside. The wind and rain whipped at her hair and clothes as she walked over to the chook house. The hen tucked neatly into the bodice of her dress, warm against her skin. Out on the road there was only twenty metres of gravel left and she waded into the dark floodwater until the tug of cold water at her knees threatened to knock her over. She grabbed hold of a tree and climbed up onto a branch, cradling the chook close to her and waiting for the lightning to show the ripples in the water running swift and muscular underneath her.

It was on the trip down south that things had started to change. She had detected a false note in Tom from the moment he came to pick them up. He drove fast along the highway, refusing to stop for water or something to eat, only pulling over for a pee break on the side of the road outside Wollongong. The three of them walked into the bush, into the smell of hot eucalyptus, twigs crackling underfoot and cars whizzing by on the highway. Allie found a tree to hide behind and she watched Tom where he stood next to Mae, looking down as she squatted and pissed onto the dirt and dry leaves. Mae's face was blank until she sensed him watching her, then she smiled and stood up, turning her bare bum to him before pulling up her underpants.

The motel was a grey cement box right on the beach. He switched off the engine and turned to look at Mae, his voice tight. 'She saw you last night.'

Mae reached for the door handle, smiling. 'Oh? Well, so what? Just say I'm some mad bitch you've never seen before.'

He grabbed her arm. 'She knows who you are and she's flipped her lid. She's gone to her mother's with the kids. And it's your fucking fault.'

'*My* fault?'

'If you didn't come prowling around in my garden like some bloody peeping tom… '

Mae stared back at him. 'Peeping at Tom.'

He was silent, then got out and slammed the car door.

The small motel room was crowded with four sagging beds. Mae changed into her swimmers as soon as Tom put their bags down and ran down the grassy dunes onto the white beach. She was like a bright crazy bird staggering across the shimmering sand in her red bikini, hands waving, shouting back at them, her voice swallowed by the sound of the surf.

Later, the weak trickle of warm water from the shower scalded Allie's sunburnt skin as she listened to them arguing through the bathroom door. Mae didn't usually talk back to Tom, but her voice was loud. When Allie came out of the bathroom, Mae rubbed cream onto her burnt back with rough hands. They sat on the grassy dune and picked at lukewarm Chinese takeaway while Mae kept going on about how wonderful it was to finally make the trip they had been planning for months. The louder she got, the quieter Tom became. Their dinner congealed in the plastic containers until the mozzies came and they went back to the hotel room. Allie lay on one of the beds and inched the rusted window open, so she could hear them outside on the balcony. She was shaken by the dismissive tone in Tom's voice. 'You did well enough from the arrangement, Mae, don't kid yourself. You could have ended it just as easily as me. It's just not working anymore, not the way you're carrying on.'

'Oh very nice, Tom. This is how you tie up eight years, huh? Just like this? Take us away to some cheap mouldy motel and call me a crazy bitch.' Mae spat out her words. 'Well don't think you can come sliming around, crawling into my bed any time you like. I couldn't stomach fucking you if the rent wasn't being paid, sweetheart.'

There was a scuffling noise then a slap and a sound like air being punched from a cushion. Mae came into the room, holding her face. She bolted the door behind her, told Allie to lock the window and disappeared into the bathroom. Allie hardly slept all night, afraid Tom would try to force his way in. Every noise woke her, footsteps outside, car doors slamming, even the waves crashing onto the beach.

He was gone in the morning but had paid the bill. They got a lift back to the city with a travelling salesman who tried to chat Mae up the whole way home.

Mae started sleeping in the day and staying up all night. Sometimes Allie would sleep in her mother's bed and she'd wake in the night and slowly reach out in the darkness, to the cool, flat sheet on Mae's side of the bed.

The last night, Allie woke to Mae's hand on her and the sound of Tom's key in the front door. 'It's him. Go down and stop him.' But he was already in the door and starting up the stairs. He smelt of the wet street outside and aftershave and alcohol. Allie wobbled sleepily, her hands outstretched to stop him like Mae had said, but he had moved her to one side and pressed her against the wall. And she had simply turned and watched him go through the door at the top of the stairs.

chapter twenty-two

The dawn light showed the damage. A carpet of twigs and branches littered Saul's lawn and a big tree on the edge of the clearing had split in two, its pale inner wood jagged and exposed.

Julia sat on the step to pull her boots on. Saul was the one she had imagined telling, even when she was a kid. But she had always anticipated feeling a great relief, an unburdening. The fact was that she had waited too long, it was too late for the telling to help Mae. She shut Saul's front door behind her and walked across the fallen debris to her car but the engine was dead.

Sitting there, her hands resting on the steering wheel, she tried to remember what had happened when Mae came back up to the house after milking, that awful morning. But she couldn't remember any morning in particular, just her mother in an apron, serving porridge in winter, cereal in summer, boiled eggs and toast. Mae always sat across from Julia, with long neat plaits, carefully sprinkling salt onto her egg and spooning it into her mouth. Mae was the one who chatted, and stole her mother's toast, and recounted the latest school gossip. Julia recalled it as if she wasn't there at all. As if there were only three in the family and she were simply a pair of eyes recording it.

Julia tried to talk to her mother about it once. She couldn't remember what she had said, but her mother had looked at her as if she was crazy. 'What are you talking about, Julia? What's wrong with you?' Every day Julia woke and was going to tell someone and every day she didn't. Then Mae was gone and she had missed her chance. But she paid for it. By the time her father died she had paid for it.

Saul appeared on the verandah, his clothes crumpled. He leaned against the verandah post and looked down at her where she sat in the car, the door open. She wanted him to say something, to acknowledge what had passed between them in the night. Eventually she spoke. 'The car won't start.'

'I think you left the headlights on.' He stepped off the verandah and started towards the shed. 'I'll get the jumper leads.'

Julia shook her head. 'I don't think it will recharge. It was dying anyway. I have a new battery at home. Will you give me a lift?' Tears pricked at her eyes as she flicked the useless headlight switch off.

He nodded, 'Sure.'

He drove slowly up the narrow track until they came upon a fallen tree blocking their way. He went back for a chainsaw and she stood to one side while he cut through the thick trunk. The noise of the saw and the tang of fresh-cut wood reminded her of taking afternoon tea up to the mill. She and Mae spent every Saturday at their grandmother's house, learning to cook. Then the three of them would walk to the mill, a basket over their grandmother's arm, the girls taking turns to hold her free hand. Julia's grandfather and uncles would stop the saws to come and eat slices of butter cake and date scones with their milky tea, while powdery sawdust drifted from their hair and eyebrows.

As Saul sliced the trunk into segments, the thick brown bark fell away in curves, exposing the tender inner skin of the tree, its wood folded like Julia's own belly that she ran her hands over in bed at night. Neal loved her body. He never said so, but she knew. She squeezed her eyes tight against the image of her father and Mae, his hands gripping her, pushing her down into the hay, even though she was as limp as a rag doll.

Saul turned the saw off and rested it on the tree trunk. 'Didn't your mother know, Julia? She must have known.'

Julia bent to roll a piece of trunk off the track. 'Why must she have known? No-one could imagine it unless they saw it.'

He grunted as he heaved a branch into the lantana thicket.

She stroked the smooth tree bark, her fingers tracing the undulations. When her mother was dying, she became so angry at Julia's father that she couldn't bear to be in the same room as him. Her mother moved to the narrow bed in the sunroom and gave up looking after him. That was when Julia had to take over washing him every day, gagging at the sight of his shrivelled old penis and wasted body.

'Mae mentioned it on the phone, Saul. You know, when she rang me that night.'

He straightened up. 'She did?'

'I was so bloody angry at her because it's only the second time she's called me in fifteen years and it was to ask a favour. And I said, why should I go when I'd waited years for her to call. She said the only reason she'd stayed, the only reason she hadn't left the valley before she did, was to keep him from me. When he had the accident, she figured I was safe from him.' Julia dusted her hands on her pants. 'So how's that? She didn't stay for you, Saul, she stayed for me.' She wiped roughly at her tears. 'She stayed for me.'

He got back into the ute and started the engine.

Julia got in. 'She thought he was going to die when the tractor rolled. When she came up for his funeral she told me that when she got to Sydney, she found herself a church and went in and knelt down and prayed he would die.'

They drove past his father's house where the dogs peered out from the dripping eaves of their shelter and a dark sally wattle tree lay shattered across the lawn. The creek was still running fast and high but had dropped, leaving grasses and bushes brutally flattened and muddy rubble over the road. The air in the car was damp and stale.

'You won't tell anyone will you?' Julia said. 'It's too much for Allie to hear.'

'You're going to tell her, though?'

She was silent.

He shook his head and slowed to drive over a hump of gravel left by the flood. 'She's living in a bloody fantasy world Julia. Now she thinks it's the poor bastard from the Show. You can't let her keep believing that.'

'It's not as easy as all that.'

'I think it is that easy, because it's the truth.' He stopped at the flooded causeway and opened his car door. 'But it's your business. I don't want to be part of it.'

Julia watched him wade out into the water . She wound down her window and called to him, 'You are part of it. You're part of it all, Saul. You chose that when you slept with her.'

He got back in and drove forward slowly. 'Okay, so if I'm part of it, I think she should be told.'

Julia looked out at the foaming brown water rushing up the side of the car. 'What if I'd told you? Back then. What would you have done?' The car surged forward as it climbed out of the creek.

He bounced his palm on the steering wheel. 'I would have helped her. I would have taken her away.' He steered up Julia's driveway, his tyres slipping on the mud. 'I want to talk to Allie about what happened yesterday. I want it to come from me not you.'

Julia reached for the door handle. 'Listen, I am the one who will decide when she is told about her father. All right?'

'Oh yeah, fine, Julia. You're the boss.'

She got out of the car. 'So, just talk to her and then leave us alone. Just talk and go, Saul. I'll ride the motorbike back with the battery later when the creek drops.'

chapter twenty-three

Saul stood on the front path, waiting for Julia to reach the lower paddocks, where she dropped onto her knees and started digging around a tree. He climbed the steps to the verandah, looking carefully at the house, at every nail that had been driven in by Mae's father, every cladding board fixed in place with his hands. The man had always towered over Saul, with his barrel chest and legs planted wide.

Inside, the house was silent except for the ticking of a clock and water dripping from the gutters. There was a branch sticking through a broken window in the living room, towels crumpled on the floor to soak up the rain, and shards of glass piled neatly on a piece of newspaper. He looked into Mae's old bedroom, but it was empty, clothes strewn around the room and the bedclothes messed up. She had taken him in there once, when her father was away, and he had been surprised how austere the room was. He sat down on her old bed and remembered the smile on her face as she ran her hand along the tightly tucked bed cover and around the hospital corners, mocking how neat it was. She could have told him in that instant, she could have turned to him right there in her room and told him.

A distant cow mooed and a chainsaw whined somewhere down the valley. He passed Julia's bedroom and saw Allie and Petal asleep in the high double bed. Petal lay with her limbs sprawled, a long tanned thigh exposed. Allie was twisted in the sheet, her legs tucked up. He stood in the doorway, examining her soft face, trying to see Mae's father in her.

'Saul?' She opened her eyes and looked at him with an unsmiling, steady gaze. Petal was motionless, her face slack with sleep.

He whispered, 'Can I talk to you, Allie?'

She nodded.

He went out onto the front verandah and sat on the top step. The sunlight seemed weak and pale after the storm. He could see Julia down with her trees, banging stakes into the ground.

Allie came to sit beside him. She had wrapped herself in a white sheet. The cicadas suddenly started singing, a wall of noise. She stretched her legs out. 'Where do the cicadas go when it rains? Do they hide somewhere?'

'I don't know. Perhaps under a leaf?' He took a breath. 'Julia wants me to stay away from you.'

'What do you mean stay away from me?' She hesitated and then reached out and touched his forearm.

He took her hand and enclosed it in his own two. She had a familiar sweet earthy smell and he was not sure if he was remembering it from yesterday or from years before with Mae. Julia was watching them from down the paddock.

He squeezed her hand. 'I'm a lot older than you, and she reminded me of that.'

'It's none of her business! Why are you even taking any notice of her?'

He could see tears rising in her eyes. 'I just feel like… it wasn't something that was thought out and it was very sweet, you were very sweet…' He heard how patronising he sounded. 'I don't think I was clear, I was still caught up in stuff around your mother… I wasn't clear and that's not fair to you.'

She lifted her chin and leaned away from him. 'So you imagined you were in bed with my mother?' She pulled her hand from his.

'No, not exactly… well yes, I guess that part of me did, it just confused things for me.'

She stood up, shaking her head. 'No,' her voice was quiet, 'I don't believe you.'

She was so like Mae, the way she stared back at him, unblinking, waiting. It used to disconcert him, how adult and contained Mae was. 'Julia's right, you know. It wasn't appropriate in the circumstances. I wasn't being responsible…' Oh God! He sounded so pompous. 'I'm sorry. I'm really sorry for messing things up like this. Anyway, Julia more or less forbids me to see you.'

'And you are so obedient?'

'Well, there's the question of the law. You're fifteen.' And only just turned fifteen. What the hell had he been thinking?

She turned and started to walk away, across the muddy yard, the sheet trailing on the ground.

'Don't Allie. Don't just run away. Come back.'

'What for?' She turned around, her cheeks flushed and eyes wide. 'No-one tells the truth around here. At least be honest, if you're scared of the cops, or if you're scared of Julia then say so. Were you or Julia ever going to tell me about Mae? How she died? Or were you going to let me go on and on, not knowing? I should have been the first to know, before you, before her.' She jabbed her finger down the hill towards Julia.

'I didn't know until the night of your birthday!'

'Exactly.' She dropped the sheet and walked down the driveway in her crumpled cotton dress and bare feet.

'Hey!' He stood up and walked after her. 'You're right, you should have been the first to know. And you know, I am afraid, afraid of myself and how I've confused you and Mae in my head. That's the truth, and I'm sorry. I'm sorry that that's the truth.'

She shook her head at him and walked away.

Saul sat back on the step, then lay on the damp verandah boards and shut his eyes. The nails sticking out of the wood dug into his back. What he hadn't said was that he was most afraid of the desire that he still felt for her. He banged his fist onto the verandah. He felt like a teenager. He was still the teenager who wouldn't have been able to handle it if Mae had told him. It was clear to him that he wouldn't have known what to do and that Mae must have realised that. He couldn't stop thinking of what Julia had seen. The image, stark in his mind, didn't fit with the peace of the morning after a flood. But the fact of it had always been there. Every moment he had been with Mae, it was under the surface, the whole time. He hadn't known Mae at all.

He sat up and watched Julia coming up the paddock,

swishing through the high weeds. Mae should have told him. He should have known.

chapter twenty-four

She was running like her mother used to. Mae would jump on any train or bus that came along or she would hitch a lift with strangers. She used to say that she liked to keep moving, going somewhere, even if it was just around and around in circles.

The woman who picked up Allie didn't try to make conversation, she didn't even ask where she was going. She just swept the old newspapers and balls of wool off the passenger seat and turned the radio on. When they reached the outskirts of town she slowed and pulled up outside her great-grandmother's house. 'This is where you'd be going, then?'

'Yes, thank you.'

The old woman came to the door in a dressing-gown. 'Oh, hello dear. Come in.'

The house smelt of toast and wet clothes. Her great-grandmother walked to the back door. 'I'm just clearing up the backyard.' Allie followed her across the squelching lawn.

'Dan did some cleaning up before he went to work, but it was a rough storm, that one.' Branches had fallen into the garden, crushing plants and gouging holes in the lawn. The old woman struggled with a branch. 'I'm sorry we had to leave early the other night. We only just made it back across the bridge as it was. Here, grab the end of this, will you. Did Julia drop you off?'

'No. I came in on my own.' Allie gripped the grainy wet bark.

'Oh.' She looked up at Allie. 'How do you get on with Julia?'

Allie was silent, then said, 'She doesn't talk to me about some... things.'

The old woman nodded. 'Apparently she and her father hardly spoke a word in his last years. Someone I know did some nursing, you know community nursing, up at the house before he died and told me that he and Julia barely said a word to each other. She's never been a great conversationalist, I guess, even when she was a little girl. And he was such a surly man. But so handsome before the accident. So handsome.' She wiped her hands on her dressing-gown. 'Oh, this will have to wait for Dan. Come inside, dear.'

She washed her hands at the kitchen sink. 'She was taken in by his looks, Bess was. He didn't charm the boys though. They were set against her taking up with him. A no-hoper, a drifter.' She tied an apron over her dressing-gown and started slicing a loaf of bread. 'We did give him the poorest piece of land, you know. Julia was right, but she shouldn't have brought it up. We didn't have enough to go carving up the best bits of it. All my boys except Dan had to move away, find their own land or get town jobs, while their sister's husband worked a piece of their family land. And look what happened in the end, we couldn't really keep going with what we had.' She poured boiling water into the teapot and dropped a slice of bread into the toaster. 'Fried or scrambled?'

'I don't mind.' Allie watched her great-grandmother cracking the eggs one-handed like Mae used to and wondered if Julia had told the old woman. Did she carry a picture in her head, too, of the man from the ferry diving in after the mermaid? It was wrong that everyone but Allie had been intimate with Mae's last breath. The stuffy kitchen filled with the smell of burning butter. The old woman poured the bowlful of yellow eggs into the pan and Allie lay down on the lumpy couch along the kitchen wall. She tried to imagine how it would feel, that last moment, the last snatch of thought before opening your mouth and sucking a wall of water down your throat, solid into the lungs, silent coughing only drawing in more cold salty water.

'Are you all right, dear?' The old lady was standing over her, her white hair sticking out at angles. She bent down and rested her soft hand on Allie's forehead.

She looked up at her great-grandmother's flesh, at the loose skin, dry and spotted around her neck and jaw. One day the faint warmth in the old woman's hand would go cold too. The skin would desiccate and shrink from the bones, shred to dust, deep under the ground, the last atoms slowly leaking from the coffin into the heavy wet soil.

The heaped eggs glistened on the plate that the old woman put on the little table beside her. Outside, there was the sound of kids shouting and cars swishing along the wet road. Cars going somewhere. Everyone but Allie was going somewhere, everyone had a momentum and knew what they were meant to be doing.

Those last nights that her mother sat out on the roof she told Allie she wasn't running anymore. Mae had slid her fingers over the dew-damp corrugations, her long fingers slowly tracing the ripples of cool metal. 'Feel it, Allie. Perfect symmetry. It's the perfect symmetry of creation.' Once Allie sat all night on the dark roof with her mother, the city lights laid out before them, the arc of the Harbour Bridge just visible through the buildings. Mae took Allie's hand in the dark and pressed Allie's fingertips to her wrist. 'Can you feel the tick of each moment passing? Here? I've never felt each moment passing before, the way it just slides away. There's a split second when it's right there, that's the moment in its fullness. Then we can never have that moment again. It's gone, it's dead. A million deaths a day.'

Allie sat up and took a cup of tea from her great-grandmother who sat in the armchair beside her.

'Are you going to eat your eggs, dear? They're getting cold.'

Allie poked a fork into the yellow mound.

'Did your mother have chooks, Allie?'

'No. Our house is in the middle of the city. Our backyard's the size of your kitchen.'

'Oh. Somehow, I thought you had a proper house, with a garden.' She drank some tea and balanced the cup and saucer on her lap. 'This is too crowded for me, down here in town. I can hear the neighbour's toilet flush. I'd give anything to be back in the valley. Still, what can you do? I couldn't divide the farm up among the boys, and it wasn't fair for Dan to be the one getting all the benefit of the place. No, I just sold up and gave the boys a bit each, to help them on their way. Small farms just aren't viable anymore. God knows what Julia is living on, must be stringing out the last of her father's life insurance, unless she's on welfare.'

Allie drew her hand across her nose, expecting to see bright blood but there was nothing, just a faint smear of mucus. Mae wouldn't let Allie wipe the blood off her face that night down in the motel. She had pushed her away. 'Leave me alone, sweetheart.' In the morning there was a bloody stain on the white pillowcase, and as they left the room, Mae went back and turned the pillow over.

Allie closed her eyes and let the sounds wash around her, a plane passing overhead, her great-grandmother clattering dishes in the sink and the washing machine spinning in the laundry. Saul had kissed her skin so gently. He had smiled up at her and then touched his lips to her breast. She slipped her hand inside her dress and cupped the weight of her breast. It was a warm and private curve. This was the perfect symmetry of creation. Like the warmth of his body the length of hers.

She looked up to where her great-grandmother was scooping a mass of pale bread dough out onto the floured table. 'What was Saul Philips like when he was younger?'

'Saul? Oh, he was a sweet boy you know. Sweet little boy. Actually he was a little girlish when he was young, not that you'd know it now. His father let his hair grow long and curly, because the boy wanted it. But it looked kind of funny. And his clothes were often too small, his father didn't think to buy him new clothes.' She started kneading the bread, leaning her weight onto the table. 'Apparently he did all the cooking at home after his mother died. He baked cakes and boiled up corned beef, the whole thing. I remember he was just wretched when she died, poor mite.'

The yeasty smell of bread dough filled the room, moist, fecund. Allie ran her hand down over her breasts to her belly. Her body felt super-heated and sweat was soaking her dress. Their skin had felt like it would melt together with the heat and sweat. Mae had once told her that the moment of sex she liked best was just as the penis slipped in, when the empty space filled. Allie knew she could go back and make him do it again, it was so easy the first time and she had seen the softness in his eyes as they sat on the verandah steps and he tried to tell her that it was wrong. She wished that he had stood up to Julia, that he had stood up to her because he wanted Allie more than anything else. Her before all else.

The old woman slapped the mass of dough down on the table. 'He went a bit odd after he and Mae broke up. He left a wire thing on Bess's verandah, a kind of wire sculpture of a heart, you know, a love heart, but it was all wrapped in barbed wire. They never showed it to Mae. It was a nasty tangle of rusty barbed wire. I think it made him a little crazy, what happened.' She sighed. 'I think it made us all a little crazy.'

'You would have to be crazy to kill yourself, wouldn't you?'

The old woman leaned on the table and considered her before saying, 'You're talking about your mother?'

Allie nodded.

'Did Julia tell you?'

'I overheard her.'

The old woman sat down at the table. 'Oh dear… You know, no-one knows for certain. It may be that it's not true, I mean, they don't really know.'

Allie could barely speak, her throat was closing. 'No. They're right.' If her throat closed completely, she wouldn't be able to breathe.

'Here.' Her great-grandmother came over and sat on the couch beside her, and pulled her into a tight hug with floury hands. Her apron was damp and she had a musty smell.

The back door opened and Julia stepped inside, kicking her boots out the door. 'I thought you might be here.'

The old woman stroked Allie's hair. 'She's got a fever, Julia, feel her temperature.'

Julia's face loomed large over her, the bony nose and lank hair. Her hand was heavy on Allie's forehead.

'Don't touch me Julia!' She brushed her aunt's arm away. 'You had no right to go and talk to him. It's none of your business.'

They moved her to the bed in the spare room, onto the cool, musty sheets. She wondered if Julia looked for evidence of Saul on her body as she tied Allie's sweat-soaked hair up into a band and peeled off her dress. Her great-grandmother sponged her with tepid water.

She drifted in and out of sleep, the heat moving through her. Julia sat in the dappled sunlight by the window and as the afternoon passed, the light faded until it was nearly dark in the small room.

Her aunt's voice was quiet. 'I'm sorry I didn't tell you what the police said. I didn't think it was the right time. I couldn't… I didn't think you could handle knowing that about your mum… No-one ever looked after her. That's all I'm trying to do. Look after you. I'm trying to second-guess what she would want… but you were right when you said I don't really know her. So it's just mad wild guesses. I'm sorry. Just guesses.'

Allie could hear the blood pumping around her body, the squelching sound as it was propelled through her arteries. She didn't need Julia to look after her, she didn't need anyone to look after her. She was like Mae, she could get on the next train and leave them all behind.

'Even when we were kids I didn't know her,' Julia said. 'Even when we slept together… did she tell you that when we were little we used to sleep in the same bed? She would crawl in with me in the middle of the night and we curled up together like spoons, until they started smacking her for it. They threatened to put her out in the back sunroom on her own. So she went back to her own bed.

'She never even told me she was pregnant. I just found out when Mum guessed. She didn't tell Saul either. The kids were whispering it up and down the school bus every single day… and she just let him find it out, so she lost him as well. It didn't have to be so complicated…'

Allie turned in the bed, her great-grandmother's nightie and the sheets under her were damp and hot. She stretched her body along the cool wall beside the bed and let it take some of the heat from her. She couldn't see her aunt's lips moving in the dim light and sometimes she wasn't sure if Julia was really talking.

'Mae understood what I wanted to do with the trees though, when she came back for Dad's funeral, when you both came back. I'd started planting them in the bottom paddocks before he died. Just planting up the far corners so no-one would notice and tell him. I even thought about moving a fence line, bringing it in so I could plant on the other side and pretend it was the forest's land. Mae was the only one to get it, other than Neal. She really understood that it's about returning to natural order. I told her that you really can recreate a rainforest in a bare paddock. It takes a hundred years, or maybe a couple of hundred years, but it happens, tree by tree by tree.' Julia's clothes rustled as she moved in her chair. 'Neal lives up near the bluff. In a little tin shack. I don't really talk to anyone about him, but you'll meet him when he comes back from up north. He collected my very first seeds for me. He wouldn't come to the house when Dad was alive, he'd just leave them down in the dairy in old jars, with little notes about what the tree was, and a sketch of how it would look when it was mature.' She leaned forward. 'How's your temperature?' Her hand was warm and steady on Allie's forehead. 'That feels better. Drink some more water.'

Allie's neck shook with the strain of lifting to drink from the glass that Julia held up. She sank back onto the bed and curled up, her back to her aunt, surprised at the comfort she felt letting Julia's words wash around her.

'Do you know who built Neal's shack originally? My father. Dad hated people to know that when he came to the valley he was a hobo. He came over to the coast after his father's farm was repossessed and he built a tin shack in the forest and got a job at Grandpa's sawmill. He bathed in the creek every evening and my mother did his laundry for him. But he would never admit to it. Mum told me.'

Allie's voice came out quiet. 'You shouldn't have gone to see him, you know. It's just between me and him, and you've scared him off.'

'He was already going to come to you and say… '

'You should never have even got involved! She wouldn't have. Mae wouldn't have. She would have let us be.'

'She wouldn't have got involved? I can hardly believe it, Allie.'

'Believe it. That's not the kind of thing she worried about.'

'Oh Allie, I don't know how to look after you.'

'I don't need looking after.'

Julia leaned forward. 'I don't want people talking about you like they used to talk about Mae. They used to say it, just because she was beautiful, you know. The men used to say it. They wanted her and she played up to them, the stupid fool. She led them on and flattered them, the old farmers, Dad's friends. She flirted with them, then she'd lie in bed at night, laughing, imitating them ogling her. And some day they'd realise that she was taking the micky out of them and they'd start to badmouth her. She was too much for the valley, you know… Sometimes I've thought she took my share of liveliness too, it's as if she got it all… ' Julia fell silent.

There was the sound of pans clanking in the kitchen

and the rumble of a male voice. It must be Dan home from work. The heat had passed and Allie felt empty and hollow, her body curled around the space inside her. She tried to conjure the sensations she felt after making love to Saul—she had been so full, bursting from her skin—but they were gone. She was as light and insubstantial as that night she stood on the stairs and faced Tom and he had moved her to one side like a paper doll. How on earth had Mae thought that Allie could stop him?

'You know… ' Allie's mouth was dry, 'I could have followed her and stopped her.'

'What do you mean? How could you have done anything?'

She shut her eyes. She could have pinned Mae to the footpath. She could have laid down on her mother's body with the weight of her own and kept her from the harbour.

Julia's voice was close. 'You once said that Mae and Tom had an argument the night before she… went out… before she drowned. What happened?' Her aunt was kneeling by the bed. 'Was he rough?'

His hands on Allie had been firm, not rough. But what were the shapes of his hands when he went in to Mae? How had their bodies collided to make the sounds that paralysed Allie where she lay in bed, fingers stuffed into her ears? 'He was rough.'

There had been such a mild look in Tom's eyes, just a casual glance up at her as he rubbed at the blood on the floor with his handkerchief, the policeman only a few metres away in the kitchen. Then he had neatly folded the hanky and put it back in his pocket, stained with the blood and grey dust from the floorboards.

'She phoned me that night, from a phone box,' Julia was whispering. 'She said she wanted me to come down, to take care of you… ' She stroked Allie's hair back from her face.

Mae in a phone box somewhere, thinking of Allie, speaking Allie's name. 'What did she say?'

'She asked me to go to Sydney, to get you and bring you back up here.'

Was she still thinking of Allie as she fitted the oars into the rowlocks and pushed off from the pier? And while she was rowing? It must have taken her hours to get out to the Heads, rowing close to the harbour shoreline, slowly passing hundreds of people sleeping in their beds and the silent yachts at private jetties.

'Did she say she was going out in the dinghy?'

'No. No… she didn't say anything like that.'

Allie had pretended to be asleep when her mother came and stood at her door. She lay there, hating Mae for asking her to stop Tom and for making her listen to it all, the crashing furniture, the thump of a body against the wall and the same old scraping of the bed. Car headlights coming down the road shone into the room and she could see the marks on her mother's face, but she didn't see the blood until the next morning. She found the half-dried drops inside her door only a few seconds before Tom did and then he was on his knees, wiping them away. The last of her mother on his handkerchief, folded into his pocket, to be washed down some laundry drain.

Allie knew that when Mae stood at her door for those few minutes, while that random scattering of drops

fell to the floor, it wouldn't have occurred to Mae to
take the four steps across the room and reach down to
wake her daughter. Because she had always done things
on her own. She had always left Allie behind. She had
always left her behind when she caught those trains to
anywhere and got off in some new country town, phoning
in the afternoon and telling Allie to go down to the
neighbour's for the night. Mae would have turned and
gone out the front door without thinking to wake her.

Julia must have left the room while Allie slept. She
woke later to darkness, and when she got up her head
was light and her feet uncertain on the floor. She opened
the bedroom door and her great-grandmother's voice
came from the kitchen. 'And why would you wait all
this time? Years and years. It doesn't make sense to me.
What are you trying to do?'

Julia's voice was faint. Allie could picture her, leaning
back in her chair, stubborn chin dropped, her voice
quiet. 'I can't believe I am the only one who had any
idea. I don't think it works like that... ' She started
mumbling and Allie couldn't make out the words.

'It doesn't work like that because it's not true, Julia.'

Their voices disappeared under the clatter of crockery
and a running tap. Allie crept down the hall, past doors
opening into dark rooms, towards the light of the kitchen.

The old woman's voice became clear, '... and it's not
fair to spread stories that could destroy a family.'

'I saw it!' Julia was almost shouting. 'With my own
eyes. How can you call it a story? Am I a liar now? I
was there.'

'Keep your voice down! You'll wake Dan and Allie.'

Allie inched further along the hall until she could

see into the kitchen and the two women sitting at the table, blue light coming from a small lamp, a mosquito coil burning on the windowsill. She leaned against the wall, her breath shaky, waiting for whatever they were going to say next. She thought of Saul's steady breath while he slept.

'You know Grandma, I'd hoped that when I told you, you would say to me, "Yes, I thought there was something going on too and I was also too afraid to do anything." I was hoping that I wasn't the only one…' Julia's chair scraped on the floor as she stood up. 'So you think the story will destroy the family, do you? I think the fact of it has already done the job. Look! I'm all that's left.'

Allie hurried back down the hall and out the door onto the wet lawn where she stood, her heart racing.

She could hear her great-grandmother going into the bathroom, the pipes clanking and the old woman muttering to herself. Allie's mouth was dry. She sat down on a lawn chair as the back door opened and light flooded onto the grass.

Julia leaned against the doorframe as she took her socks off and came down the steps and across the lawn. She sat on the chair beside Allie and opened a pouch of tobacco. 'I haven't smoked for years.' Her fingers were clumsy as she started rolling a cigarette. 'I was just thinking about how much she loved you. She told me that from the moment she guessed she was pregnant, she loved you. There was a real… ferocity in it. A fierce love.'

'What did she say to you on the phone? There must be something…'

'She asked me to go to Sydney and bring you back up here. And she wouldn't say why.'

'How did she sound?'

Julia rubbed her face. 'She didn't really sound like I remembered her, she sounded upset, kind of... distant. And she mentioned something that you really should know about. Something... I guess she meant for me to be the one to tell you. A kind of justice.' She coughed and turned on her seat to face Allie. 'Your father, I think he gave up trying to be a good man. I saw... I know who your father really is, Allie. I've always known. Your father, Mae's father, my father. It's the same man. You and I have the same father.'

In the faint light from the house, Allie watched Julia's lips forming the words and her body went quiet, all the fear suddenly drained away. She could feel each heartbeat like a slow wave moving up through her body.

Julia lit her cigarette and inhaled deeply. 'He held you once. Only once that I saw. I was minding you while Mae had a shower and he came in from outside, and took you from me and he stood there in the dining room, still in his farm clothes, all sweaty. And he cradled you in his arms and stroked your cheek.' She frowned as she lifted her hand and stroked her own face. 'He was so... tender. And Mae came out of the shower in her dressing-gown and this sound came from her and she grabbed you off him, and she never let me hold you after that. She would hardly put you down.'

'So her father is my father?' It was like listening to another voice say the words.

Julia nodded. 'It was wrong, what he did. But that doesn't make you wrong. You understand that don't you?' She looked up at the sky. 'I think she thought of you as coming only from her. And you look like it. It's as if she wished him away, willed his genes to disappear. I'm sorry… '

Allie stood up and the damp earth seemed to tilt under her bare feet. 'But there's still his blood in me.' She pinched hard at the skin of her forearm.

Julia leaned forward. 'I have his blood, so did Mae. So do you. What he did is terrible, but just the fact of being his daughter is not.'

'It *is* terrible or she would have told me! She wouldn't have lied.' She looked out over the sea of rustling sugar cane, to the high clouds, their edges lit by the moon. She felt she might float up to the clouds, her body thin as air. She would rise into the night sky, his blood draining from her, the sticky darkness streaming onto the ground.

'Allie… ' Julia stood up and laid her hand on Allie's arm.

She pulled away from her aunt and ran blindly into the dark field of sugar cane, twisting and turning between the plants, blades of cane cutting her skin, mud under her bare feet and Julia crashing through the cane behind her. She ran until her breath tore at her throat, until there was nothing to run to, just the same fields stretching to the hills. Even if she kept running all the way to the red desert, she would still have his blood in her, the blood of the faceless grandfather who had gripped her mother and rutted like a dog. She slowed and sank onto the wet earth.

Julia reached her, breathing heavily.

She could just see her aunt's pale hair and shirt in

the moonlight. 'How do you know?' Allie's voice shook. 'Why should I believe you?'

Julia sat beside her. 'I saw it.'

She gripped her knees to her chest and pressed her teeth hard into the skin of her knee. She wanted Mae's hand on her, she wanted Mae holding her and stroking her hair back. She longed to be curled around, wrapped up, spooned like a baby. 'Does Saul know?'

Julia nodded.

And she let Julia hold her shaking body together, while the wind coming down from the hills worried the tall cane around them.

chapter twenty-five

The farmhouse was dark when they got home and Petal was already asleep under the mosquito net on the verandah.

All around the house was a tremendous stillness, as if the land had been battered into silence by the flood. The faintest noise hit Allie's ears like gunshot, water dropping from the trees onto the roof, a lone cricket rasping in the bushes. She could tell Julia was awake in her own room, like Allie, lying with her eyes wide into the darkness, listening to the silence.

Allie brought her knees to her chest as if she were curled in Mae's womb again, cradled in the warm, salty sea of her mother. Perhaps Mae had tried to keep her inside that safe watery place, lying in the same bed, her hands stretched over her belly, holding her baby back while outside the rain fell and the flood waters massed.

The smell of wet earth rose through Allie's open window, carrying the faint sounds of animals burrowing and tree roots inching through the soil. The air held residue of everything that had happened at the farm, including the moment of Allie's conception, her mother spreadeagled, pinned down, that moment.

She sat up, and in the faint moonlight coming in the window, looked down at the white rectangle of bed around her. She swung her feet to the floor and hurried across the hall to the door of her aunt's dark bedroom. 'Julia?' Allie heard her sit up and fumble for the lamp.

Her aunt's face was pale and her eyes squinted against the bright light. 'Are you okay?'

'Where did it happen? Tell me what you saw.'

'Oh, Allie.' Julia lifted a hand to her face, 'No. No.'

Allie stepped into the room. 'Was it in my bed?'

'No!' Julia shook her head vehemently. 'No. Do you think I'd let you sleep there?'

'So, where?'

Julia took a breath, 'The dairy. It was in the dairy.'

Allie walked through the house and looked down to the dark outline of the old dairy building. Such a simple shape, a simple harmless shape. She opened the back door and started down the steps. The moonlight threw shadows of trees onto the paddock, and the tree trunks glowed silver, like night had become day. As she crossed the yard, her limbs moved slowly through the air as if through water.

At the dairy she pulled hard on the metal doorhandle and dragged the wooden door across the dirt. She felt around the doorframe for the light switch and three bulbs lit up the long room, with its empty stalls and feeding troughs. There was the sound of Julia coming down the steps and across the yard.

The cement floor was rough under her bare feet and she stirred the fine hay dust as she walked slowly around the room.

Julia stepped inside and pointed to the far wall, at a small door that had been boarded up with a piece of wood.

'In there?' Allie asked.

Julia nodded and took a jemmy from the wall of tools and levered the plank off the doorframe. The wood splintered and she wrenched it free with her hands.

The second room was small and windowless, stacked with wooden tea chests and old cream churns, one wall lined with shelves of paint tins and dusty bottles. Allie made herself go and stand in the middle of the room. It was so quiet in there that she could hear every quaver of her breath. The air tasted stale, like it had been trapped inside for years. She turned in a slow circle, letting her eyes run over the shapes, the corners, the angles of the room where her mother had been. Where her mother had prayed not to be.

Julia was in the doorway, the jemmy still in her hand, watching Allie. The pale girl with plaits, standing in the door, watching it happen.

And her father. Allie imagined him buckling his belt, dusting his pants down and going back to the milking.

She pushed past her aunt to get outside into the fresh air, where she stood on the muddy earth, facing the dark house, the dairy looming behind her. The air from the small room was still in her body. She bent forward and leaned her hands on her knees and drew in the cool dawn air.

Julia came to stand beside her and spoke softly, 'I'm sorry.'

She looked up at her aunt in the light spilling from the dairy door. 'Did she know that you saw it?'

'I think so.'

'But she never spoke to you about it?'

Julia shook her head.

'Who did you tell?'

Julia looked down at her hands before replying. 'I don't know how to make you understand what it was like, why I didn't tell. I was just so afraid of him. And I was young…' She turned to Allie, 'and I was weak and I regret it.'

Allie whispered, 'Do I look like him?' She touched her face, the shapes under her fingertips suddenly unfamiliar. 'Can you recognise anything of him in me?'

'Allie. Allie.' Julia's hands were around hers, bringing them down from her face. 'Stop it.' She led Allie across the yard and up the steps to the house where she took a photo album from a shelf in the kitchen. She flicked through the yellowing pages to a photo of a broadshouldered man standing in front of a tractor.

He was wearing overalls and looking straight at the camera, squinting his eyes into the sun, one hand lifted to brush the floppy fair hair from his forehead, a slight smile on his face. Allie bent down to try to see into his eyes. Her father's eyes. But they were just tiny dark marks on the skin of the photo. She touched the image and his half-smiling face was small next to her finger.

'You're not like him. There's nothing of him in you.' Julia closed the album. 'I'm like him. You and Mae take after Mum.' She traced a finger over the album cover.

'He wouldn't let me talk about Mae. But I wouldn't let him forget. I was the one person who knew and every time I looked at him, every time I brought him a meal, I made sure he knew I was thinking of it. That's why I stayed. I didn't stop it, I failed her, and staying was my way to pay.'

'So Saul didn't know?'

Julia shook her head. 'No. He found out last night.'

Allie walked to the front door.

'Where are you going?'

'To his place.'

'Let me drive you.'

'No. I want to go through the forest.'

Julia paused. 'All right. I'll be here.'

In the faint light she stepped from boulder to boulder, then stopped in the middle of the creek to look around at the mist sitting low on the water and drifting through the trees. Her father had been in the valley all along. She looked back the way she had come, towards the paddocks he had cleared and the fences he had dug into the land. He had left his mark all over the valley.

She stepped from the boulder into the creek and started wading towards the bank, the strong water rushing up her legs, soaking her clothes. She knew Mae must have longed for the moment that she would slip into the harbour. She must have rowed as fast as she could, each stroke of the oars taking her away from Allie and closer to the place where she would shed her clothes and at last, drop into the black water.

Saul was sitting on the verandah as if he were waiting for her. His dog's head was in his lap and he was lighting a cigarette. As she crossed the misty clearing, he moved his dog and stood up to lean against the railing in his pyjama bottoms and an old T-shirt. He offered a tentative smile. 'Allie.'

She climbed the steps and sat on the old couch facing him. 'So, Julia told you.'

He nodded and stubbed his cigarette into the full ashtray beside him. He came to sit beside her on the couch, his legs stretched out in the soft cotton pants, his tanned feet crossed on the verandah boards. 'Now I look back, I can see it, but I didn't know what to look for.' He turned to her. 'I just feel… sad for her that she was so alone with it.'

Allie was suddenly exhausted, her body aching and tired, her clothes wet from the creek. Mae would never have told him. She had even left it to Julia to tell Allie.

She looked out to the forest, where the sea of green was shifting in the early morning breeze and the pale sky was turning blue. 'Shouldn't you be milking?'

'He'll manage.'

She brought her knees up close to her body. 'You know, when she went rowing that night, she knew she wasn't coming back. She rang Julia and told her to go down to Sydney and bring me here. So she knew what she was going to do out on the harbour… She planned to leave me behind.' She saw Mae standing in the rocking dinghy, her feet wide for balance as she slipped her dress over her head. And she would have paused for a moment, as the breeze lifted off the water and the waves slapped the side of the dinghy, before she stepped off into the harbour.

There was just the heat of Saul's bare arm next to hers and the trees rippling and soughing around them.

'She planned for me to be the one to come back to the valley.'

He put his arm around her, warm across her shoulders. After a moment she reached up to take his arm off and lay his hand back on his thigh. And they sat looking out at the tangle of green, at the serene trees that had been there all along. Beyond the tallest trees, further down the valley, was Julia's farm. One day soon they would be able to see the tops of her trees from Saul's verandah.

chapter twenty-six

They floated in the big waterhole, two pale bodies held by the green water, arms outstretched, turning with the gentle flow of the creek. Allie let some of the water into her mouth. Every day it was less bitter. Every time she and Julia swam, there was less grief leaking from them into the water. Julia's long hair was silky on Allie's arm, and the cool flesh of her aunt's leg brushed hers. The trees rose high either side of the creek, the big green leaves silhouetted against the sky.

From above, from up near the treetops, there would be the shapes of the two women floating down the creek through waterhole after waterhole, past boulders, under bridges, travelling the spine of the valley. And floating ahead of them, the grey cladding boards from the dairy building. Ten of them every day, levered off, carried to the creek and launched. The weathered strips of old hardwood, twisting and turning in the eddies, slipping over rapids, sometimes wedging between boulders to wait for the next flood to lift them and carry them away. They would float all the way to the sea, to the wide salty sea.

acknowledgments

For support and critique, thanks to Laura Jan Shore, Jesse Blackadder, Millie Connolly, Emma Hardman, Hayley Katzen, Dan Phillips, and Matt Ottley. For early encouragement, thanks to the Northern Rivers Writers' Centre, Jill Eddington, the Beach Hotel, the *Byron Shire Echo*, and Inez Baranay. Thanks to Annette Barlow, Collette Vella, Catherine Milne, Briony Cameron, and everyone at Allen & Unwin. For the G4 and the Santa Cruz writing space, thanks to Joel Olinger. Big thanks to Pippa Masson and Fiona Inglis from Curtis Brown. And my gratitude and appreciation to all at MacAdam/Cage—Khristina Wenzinger, Melanie Mitchell, and Julie Burton, with particular thanks to David Poindexter.